DREAM

Lucas Colmar

Contents

Chapter 1

Lucy Monroe sat in her car watching the rain as it covered her windshield in a sheet of water. Her oldest and best friend, Thomas Kane, had asked her to meet him at one of the coffee shops in town at a ridiculously early hour. She knew it was due in part to his busy schedule, but it was also because he knew she hated going into town. The people of Belfort, Louisiana, had never embraced Lucy or anyone in the Monroe family.

She reached up and pulled her woolen hat lower over her head of silver gray hair, or the mark of the devil as some in the town referred to it. It was in fact, a very rare genetic trait that had been passed down through the generations. She wasn't an albino; she just had silver hair. However, now it was trendy, or at least it was in the big cities, in Belfort though it was still the mark of the devil.

The trait, along with the gift, as her grandmother referred to it, generally skipped a generation and her mother, Faith Monroe, had been born with thick black hair that Lucy had always envied, but it was the only thing for which she envied her mother. She was a useless soul, who had lost herself to drugs and men at a very young age.

Lucy's attention was caught by Thomas's bright red truck as it pulled into the parking spot next to her little, beat up car that was at least two decades old. Cutting her engine, she opened the door and got out quickly, slamming it hard behind because it was the only way to make sure that the door stayed closed. She then headed for the door of the café without looking to see if Thomas was behind her, knowing he was.

He bumped into her as she stopped in the doorway of the coffee shop to assess the situation. Only a few brave souls were sitting at the tables, and most of them paused in what they were doing as they caught sight of her. Pretending that they weren't there, she moved to a table at the very back of the restaurant while Thomas moved to the counter to order them their drinks, a tea for Lucy and a coffee for him. She kept her back to the room and sat with her hands on the table in front of her, not looking at anyone as she stared out of the window into the wet darkness.

"Thanks for meeting me, Lucy," Thomas said as he slid into the seat across from her.

"Does Hope know?" Lucy asked, reaching for her tea, and wrapping her hands around it.

"Yes, I told her." He nodded as he let his gaze slide across the people in the café, unafraid to meet their eyes.

"How did she take it?" Lucy looked up at Thomas, gauging the honesty in his answer.

The twisting of his mouth and the red on his cheeks let her know that she hadn't taken it well. Hope, Thomas's very pregnant wife, had never liked Lucy, she believed, like everyone else in the town, that Lucy was evil. She was also jealous of Lucy's and Thomas's friendship and felt threatened by it. It was the main reason that Lucy made a point of seeing as little of Thomas as possible over the last two years.

"She'll come around," Thomas insisted.

Lucy gave him a sad smile, Thomas had always believed the best about everyone, and she was thankful for it because without it he never would have been her friend, and other than her grandmother he was her only friend.

"So why did you get me out of bed at this ungodly hour?" she asked, the subtle play on words was not lost on Thomas as he gave her a grin. Thomas had always gotten her dry wit that went over most people's heads.

"You know the LeClair mansion?"

"Sure, we used to run around there as kids." Lucy nodded, remembering that it was the only place that she and Thomas could safely play together because all the other kids were too afraid to go near the site. It had been their playground, and she had a lot of fond memories of the times they had spent there.

Now, looking back, her lack of fear was probably another reason that all the kids had been afraid of her as well.

"Have you heard of a man named Zebadiah Abbott?" He watched her as she stirred her tea, waiting for it to cool.

"No, why? Should I have?" Thomas knew about her gift, he believed in it, but he wasn't sure how it worked, and to be honest, neither was Lucy.

"He is a very wealthy businessman out of New Orleans and he bought the LeClair mansion."

Lucy nodded, remembering that the house had recently changed owner-ship. "Is he going to tear it down?" The thought saddened Lucy, and it was a beautiful old house with an old soul.

Thomas smiled like he had won the lottery, and it caught Lucy off guard. She stopped stirring her tea, and her eyes narrowed as she waited to hear the rest. Thomas was notorious for getting them into trouble, and that smile was generally the precursor to it every time.

"No, he is doing a full restoration of the property. He's already hired two different contractors, and they both failed and packed up and left within a month!"

"Thomas!" Lucy said, excited for him. Thomas had been in business as a contractor for over five years, but he had a hard time finding work locally, and Lucy truly believed it was because of his association with her. He denied it, but she didn't believe him for a minute. "Did you get the job!" she hissed in excitement.

He nodded, his eyes dancing. "I'm going to sign the contract today, but I'll need your help."

"How?"

"The house likes you, and I need you there. Also, there is a ton of wood-work in the interior and a lot of built-ins that need restoration, and I know that you can do both. You'll be the lucky charm that allows me to finish the job," he insisted.

Lucy's passion and job was restoring old furniture, and she loved what she did, bringing long forgotten things of beauty back to life was soothing to her soul, but she only received the occasional order from an acquaintance that ran an antique shop, so the idea of steady work doing what she loved was thrilling. "You played in that house just as much as I did, it knows you just as well." Lucy shook her head, dismissing the idea, even though she was pleased by the notion of them being back in the house together. "Besides, I don't think Hope would go for it."

"I already told Hope it was a done deal, and I'm not working on the house without you Lucy." His eyes met hers across the table. "You need the work just as much as I do, and you know it."

Lucy sipped her tea and looked out the window. She did, things were tight with her and her grandmother, and if she didn't find a job soon she would have to go back to the big city to find one.

She caved. "Since your forcing me to do this, when do we start?" She turned to look at him, her light silver grey eyes meeting his soft brown ones, and a quick flash of his future filled her vision, blocking Thomas's excited gaze. She quickly saw Thomas, living in a large house, accepting an award, and wearing a suit. "It's the right choice Thomas," she assured him as she blinked away the vision.

He took a deep breath and smiled. "Thank you, Lucy!"

They talked a little more about the job, but when a steady stream of customers started to arrive, they both knew that it was time for Lucy to leave before someone took notice of her. They parted ways, making plans to meet at the house that evening before the both disappeared out of the side door.

Chapter 2

Lucy parked her car on the edge of a dirt road that ran alongside a large brick wall. She didn't know why she felt the need to stop there instead of pulling into the drive that was less than fifty feet in front of her, but it was a gut feeling that said she needed to approach the old house on foot. She got out of her old car while noting that the air around her was utterly still. To her left was open marshland that led to the river, and to her right was the large brick wall that surrounded the LeClair house, an antebellum mansion built in the 1840s, well before the civil war.

Following the wall, Lucy stopped in the drive, looking at the massive house before her. The gates that had once kept people out were long gone, and there was an air of neglect and sadness to the home.

Checking her watch, she realized that she had at least ten more minutes before Thomas was supposed to meet her, so she turned her attention back towards the building in front of her.

Slowly, she started up the drive, taking in the massive columns and wide porches that would protect the house in a storm or from the heat of the summer. Since she and Thomas had spent so much time in the house as kids, she knew what the inside looked like; she also knew that there was a large hill behind the house that led down to the river. The owner designed the house so that it sat in the u-bend of the river, and this allowed for it to catch the crosswinds no matter which way the wind was blowing.

She walked towards the porch, pausing as if to ask for permission to approach her. The house had a soul; she could feel it just as she could when she was a girl.

The house wanted salvation, and she wanted a family to live in her and love her. Lucy reached out and placed her hand on one of the columns, rubbing it soothingly, as if to tell her she was alright and that everything would soon be better.

A car pulled into the drive at a dangerous rate of speed and braked hard at the foot of the broad steps that led to the porch above. Lucy recognized it as a local police car, and she knew the man who was getting out if it. It was Joel Bradley. Joel had been harassing her since they were kids. When they were younger, she had suffered a child's harassment; pulling pig-tails, making fun of her hair, or her family. Now, as an adult, it was a completely different type of bullying, and it scared her.

"Why Lucy Monroe, I haven't seen you around for quite a while," Joel said as he exited his car, slamming the door behind him, his thick southern drawl antagonistic.

"I try to stay out of trouble," Lucy responded in her deep husky voice while trying to force a polite smile to her face

"If that's true, then why are you trespassing right now?" He looked up at the house behind her as he placed a hand on his handcuffs in a threatening manner.

"I'm not trespassing, I was invited to meet Thomas Kane here," she informed him, moving further up onto the porch as if the house would protect her.

"That's funny, I don't see Thomas here, and even if I did he would also be trespassing," Joel drawled, stepping onto the porch, following Lucy.

Lucy didn't say a word. She knew that anything she tried to say would only make matters worse. He was looking for a reason to harass her, and he thought he had found it.

"Now, perhaps we can make a deal," he said as he let his gaze travel over her.

There was nothing spectacular in the way that she looked. She had tucked her short-cropped silver hair under her ball cap and, because it was early spring and still cold, she was wearing a thermal shirt under her baggy work overalls with a flannel shirt over the top. Her work boots added an extra few inches to her small stature, but not enough to intimidate Joel.

"There's no need to make a deal Joel, I'm not doing anything wrong," insisted Lucy as she silently prayed for Thomas to arrive.

"You're up to something Lucy Monroe, even if it's not trespassing. You Monroes are always up to no good." His hand reached out towards her, and Lucy stepped back just as Thomas's truck pulled into the drive and parked right next to Joel's squad car.

"Joel!" Thomas greeted as he jumped out of his truck.

"Thomas," Joel greeted in return. "I was just checking on things here, making sure that Lucy wasn't trespassing." Lucy couldn't help but note that his whole demeanor changed at Thomas's arrival. Joel had always been a coward. He looked over Lucy one last time; his look implied that he would catch up with her sooner or later.

"She's not trespassing, we have a meeting," Thomas confirmed as he climbed the steps, pulling out his key and opening the door, proof that he was there legitimately. "If you don't mind, I don't have much time, so we need to get started." He held out his arm, welcoming Lucy past him, and she wasted no time in rushing past him and into the safety of the house.

Thomas didn't wait for Joel to leave. Instead, he joined Lucy in the cold foyer of the house, closing the door behind them.

Joel would probably have it all over town that Lucy and Thomas had had a secret meeting planned, and he would put the worst possible spin on it.

"It looks like I got here just in time?" Thomas said as he threw an arm around her shoulders.

"You always manage to somehow." Lucy smiled, not bothering to remind him what would happen once Joel returned to town.

It would be one more thing for people to hate her for, and she should be used to it after living with it for over twenty-six years.

Chapter 3

"So, how did your meeting go today? Did you get your contract signed?" Lucy casually asked as she walked up to the ornate newel post of the grand staircase. "Why do people do this?" she complained as she tried to scrape away some of the loose white paint that covered the original wood. "They ruin the wood and the history."

"It's all about taste Lucy, and different people have different tastes. Some people don't appreciate the old patina that this wood gets after generations of use, they want to lighten things up."

"Then they should by a new house, not an old one!" Lucy insisted as she walked into the drawing room, it was stunning, or it had been. Someone had once again painted over all the woodwork on the walls, ceiling, and built-in cabinetry, but thankfully the floor hadn't been touched.

"You'll be happy that it's a full restoration then Lucy, and that Zebadiah Abbott has very deep pockets. I had a verbal confirmation that I am to spare no expense in bringing her back to what she once was," Thomas assured her.

Lucy felt herself get excited at the prospect. "All of the woodwork? You realize that it will take at least six months, maybe a year to do it all?" Almost an entire year that she wouldn't have to worry about money.

"Yes," he agreed, watching her closely.

"I sense there is a 'but' in there Thomas," she said warily.

"The house, I need you to read it and tell me what went wrong last time," Thomas said it in a rush as if it would make it easier to say. At Lucy's passive face he rushed on, afraid that he had insulted her. "I know that I have never asked you to use your gift Lucy, but I need it. There have been two other firms that have worked on this house, and neither one lasted a month. Things happened, unexplainable things that scared the workers away. I want to know what happened, and what I can do so that those things don't happen to me."

"And you think I can tell you that?" Lucy asked. She wasn't insulted, she knew what a job like this would mean for Thomas. It would not only bring him much needed cash flow, but it would also make his name in the business, and with a baby on the way, it would be a relief.

Lucy gave a small smile. "Fine, Thomas, I'll help you, provided I get to do all of the wood restorations in the house, but don't worry, I'll charge a fair price."

"I didn't doubt you would," Thomas grinned, relieved. "You'll have to be on site most of the time, and I think having you here will put a lot of the men at ease."

Lucy snorted. "That's rich, considering if it was anywhere else in this town they wouldn't want me near them." Lucy walked over to the mantle and touched it, running her hand across the scratched-up wood.

Thomas watched her silently as she moved around the house, peeking into all the rooms and walking around the upstairs balcony, looking out over the river.

"There are a few things that you can do that I think might help the job run smoothly." She walked back into the house, closing the door and starting down the stairs. The house hadn't talked to her, even though that was probably what people would think. She had empathized with the old girl, thinking about how she would feel if she were an old lady living in today's world. She was following her heart.

"Number one, the house is not haunted, that's important. She, the house, wouldn't stand for it." Lucy waved her hand around her head. "She's a serious old girl, and she does not appreciate shenanigans unless they're from children." Lucy smiled. "She loves children, which probably is why she let us play here as kids."

Thomas smiled and shook his head. "You're talking about her as if she was real."

"She is, very real." Lucy looked at him without a trace of humor. "You won't succeed if you don't take this seriously."

He held up his hands in surrender. "You're the boss!"

"Number two, old-school, she doesn't like the sound of power or pneumatic tools, keep those away from the house, build as much offsite as you can and bring it in and install it with old-school tools, those she recognizes and appreciates."

Thomas groaned. "Do you know how much time we'll lose!"

"If you want to finish, this is what you'll have to do. Number three, everyone needs to park outside of the wall or in the back. She is very into appearances, and she doesn't want port-o-lets and cars littering up her yard, keep a clean site."

Thomas grumbled under his breath, and Lucy realized she was enjoying herself. She was glad to speak on behalf of the house, even though she honestly didn't know if she was making it up as she went or not. That was how her gift worked. It was often just a vision or feeling that led her.

"Number four, no cursing, catcalling, or other lewd behavior. You have to behave as if she was your grandmother with a sensitive head." Lucy squeezed Thomas's arm.

"Do you know how impossible that's going to be with my crew?"

"Just let everyone know that I told you that this is how it has to be, and if they don't follow the rules they won't have jobs because the house will kick them out." Lucy knew that everyone already thought she was a witch or something similar, so they would probably believe everything that she said.

Thomas nodded, leading the way out the front door, closing it behind him.

"Thomas, do you know how wonderful this project will be?" She reached out and touched his arm once more, looking at her hand as it rested against his red jacket, and just as she had in the café that morning, she saw his future clear as day, this was her God-given gift. She could see the moment a person made a decision that changed their future, whether it was for better or worse, and right now, for Thomas, it was for the better.

She saw his business grow, the house finished, his wife happy, and a boat. She smiled at the last bit; he had always wanted a boat.

"What do you see Lucy?" he asked nervously, knowing she had a vision, recognizing the signs.

"I see a boat, a big boat if you say yes to the job. It will be hard, but you'll succeed."

"As long as I do as you say," he teased.

"Yep!" She laughed as she walked down the steps towards her car. "Let me know when we start." She walked a few steps before she stopped and turned to look at him. "What's the name of the man who purchased the house again?" She had a sudden urgency to hear the name once more.

"Zebadiah Abbott, he's out of New Orleans, I told you this morning, remember?" Thomas called before climbing into his truck.

Lucy paused, it wasn't a name that she recalled having heard before, but there was something familiar about it. "Zebadiah, Zeb," she said the name softly, and a shiver chased its way up her spine at the intimate sound of it on her lips. "Zeb," Lucy repeated it and felt her breath catch, and her cheeks burn, that had never happened before. "Abbott," she said the name for a change, but there was nothing with it.

Lucy waved to Thomas as she climbed into her car and started the engine, and when she got halfway down the road, she repeated it once more. "Zeb."

She slammed on her breaks, her face heating up again as she heard her name laughingly called by an unrecognizable male voice, and it felt as if someone had wrapped a warm blanket around her.

Shaking, she let up off the brake and drove slowly the rest of the way home, wondering who Zebadiah Abbott was and why his name had such a strong effect on her.

Chapter 4

"I'm pleased with the progress," Zebadiah said as he stood next to Thomas and his assistant foreman, Steve Shepard, while they looked over at the house. "I thought you would have been a little bit further along, but what has been done is excellent work."

Thomas couldn't tell how upset he was at the fact that they were behind because his face was devoid of any emotion, it might as well have been made of stone. "Thank you, we're moving at a steady pace and are still on schedule," Thomas assured the intimidating man next to him.

Zebadiah Abbott made Thomas nervous, and his gut told him that he was not a man to cross, but he was fair and the few problems that had cropped up in the last two months had been dealt with easily enough.

They were now into June and the temperature and humidity were starting to rise, making it harder to get certain things finished. They should have started in the winter, but Thomas had explained all of this to Mr. Abbott and he had seemed to understand, although he was a hard man to read so he couldn't be sure.

"Is there anything that you need that you don't have?" He turned to look at Thomas, his eyes hard as he waited for an answer.

Thomas was a tall man at six foot, but Zebadiah Abbott was taller, and even though he didn't tower above him it felt as if he did; probably because he didn't have an ounce of fat on him and he was all muscle which made him seem larger than he was.

"No, I have everything that I need, thankfully there have been very few problems with our supply delivery." Thomas missed Abbott's small nod of approval, and he had no clue that Abbott had made sure that there would be no problems.

"I'm still mystified as to how the two firms before you couldn't last two weeks, yet you've managed to last two months?" He looked at Thomas, silently demanding an answer.

Thomas opened his mouth intending to explain by using vague terms such as scheduling and leadership, but Steve cut him off before he could speak. "Oh, that's because we have Lucy?" he said with a nod, oblivious to Thomas's warning look. Zebadiah didn't miss it though.

"Lucy?" he asked, appearing to focus on Steve and not Thomas, even though he was more interested in Thomas's angry reaction.

Steve nodded. "Yep, she talks to the house and makes sure that she has everything that she wants," Steve said as he rolled up the plans they had been looking at earlier. He was a short man with a large bald spot, and he was sweating profusely.

"She, as in the house?" Zebadiah asked.

"Lucy said that we should treat her like we would our Grandmother, and that everything would be fine. The reason that the other crews were run off was because they weren't respectful enough."

Thomas looked at Mr. Abbott, noting that his face was still as blank as a stone, making it hard to judge his reaction to Steve's explanation.

"So, my house is haunted?"

Steve shrugged. "Lucy says no, that the house wouldn't stand for it."

"How does Lucy know all of this?" Zebadiah's calm reaction inspired Steve's confidence.

"She's a witch," Steve explained, but as he realized what he had said he looked at Thomas, who looked at him with enough anger to make him step back. "Sorry, just a joke. I'll go put these plans up in the box," he said as he scurried away.

Thomas caught Zebadiah watching him closely and realized that his anger showed clearly on his face, so he quickly pulled himself together.

"Let's go take a look at what's going on inside," Zebadiah suggested in an even voice that showed little concern over Steve's revelation.

******

Lucy listened to the blond woman drone on and on to her redheaded friend, Cecelia Nash, a girl that she and Thomas had grown up with, about how the house was the worst thing ever, and that there was no way that she would be living in it once she married Zebadiah. She would let him think that she was going to be happy in the old relic, but once the house was finished and the ring was on her finger, she was done.

The blond woman, whose name Lucy couldn't remember, turned towards her with a frown, as if she had just remembered that Lucy was there. With a quick glance at her baggy paint covered overalls, work boots, and ballcap, she shrugged, as if to say she was a non-entity that wouldn't be a problem.

The blond motioned to Cecelia and they left the room together with Lucy on their heels. She was glad for once that her gift hadn't reared its unwelcomed head because there was no way that she wanted to know either woman's future.

Lucy listened as, with a little cry of greeting, the blond woman ran down the stairs to greet someone at the bottom, and Lucy watched with amusement as Cecelia's eyes grew wide with apprehension, whomever it was they made Cecelia nervous.

The blond woman's voice was joined by a deep male voice and Lucy felt her heart stop. She was sure that it was a voice that she had never heard before, but it was familiar. She stepped away from the stairs, knowing that what was coming was something that she couldn't avoid.

She listened to the man's familiar tread, though she was sure she had never heard it before. Then she watched as the man's dark head crested the banister and his sharp black eyes met hers. But she didn't see him in that moment, she saw him in the future, in love.

Her vision had him smiling as he chased two equally dark headed children up the stairs, laughing as he caught one and threw her over his shoulder. She watched as he looked over his shoulder and Lucy saw herself following him up the stairs, her smile just as broad as his, and her belly heavy with child.

That they were in love was evident, but it didn't feel as if she was watching herself. The woman she saw looked like her and sounded like her, but it wasn't her, at least it wasn't the her that existed now.

Lucy didn't know how long she stared at the man as the vision played through her head, but when she came back to reality he had moved past her and into the room behind her, and she was too afraid to turn around.

Thomas was a little slower to join them, and when he reached the top of the stairs his eyes caught Lucy's with a look of resignation as he pulled her to a corner of the hallway and out of earshot of the other three.

"Tell me," she insisted. She was blocked by his body, and thankfully, he filled her vision allowing the previous one of the man with the dark eyes to fade.

"Steve told Mr. Abbott about the house and he claimed that you were a witch." That was one good thing about Thomas, he never pulled his punches; they still hurt, but at least now she knew what to expect from Mr. Abbott.

"Thomas, aren't you going to introduce me, I assume this is Lucy?" The deep voice asked from behind Thomas, and Lucy closed her eyes at the sound of it. It was the same one she had heard in the car as she had said his name. Thomas reached up and squeezed her arm before he stepped away.

"Zebadiah Abbott, this is Lucy Monroe, Lucy is handling all of the wood restoration in the house. Lucy this is Zebadiah Abbott, this is his friend, Gianna Beckett, and you know Cecelia Nash, she sold Mr. Abbott the house."

Cecelia and Gina looked at her with haughty looks, and when Gianna reached out to take Lucy's hand in greeting Cecelia stopped her with a little shake of her head. It was subtle, and she wasn't sure if Thomas caught it, but as she turned her eyes up to meet Zebadiah Abbott's dark gaze, she knew he had.

"Ms. Monroe," he greeted, holding out his hand. Lucy really didn't want to take it, but she didn't see a way not to without being rude so she placed her hand in his.

"Mr. Abbott," she said, her voice much deeper than usual as her hand was enveloped in his, and she had a sudden vision of him standing by a window and the sound of breaking glass as he was thrown backwards. She physically jerked at the shock of the image, and when the color red filled her vision she jerked her hand away from his.

******

Zebadiah's expression didn't change as he watched her eyes dilate and he skin turn pale before she jerked her hand away. If this was a witch he was unimpressed. Although he had found it odd that Thomas had seemed so protective of her. Her small stature and baggy clothes with a ballcap pulled low was not in the least witch like, but her gray, almost sliver eyes, gave him pause. She didn't appear to be more than twenty at most.

"Would you show me some of your work?" he asked, watching her nod and then turn towards the room behind him.

"This," she had to clear her throat, and he had to admit that her deep honey tones were very sensual, "this is the first room that I've done, and I'm almost finished. There were years of paint to strip away, and I was pleased to see the intricate details that had been hidden by the many layers." She took the time to point some of them out, paying attention to the lover's knot carved into the mantel of the fireplace as she traced it with her fingers.

The room had originally been the study or library, and the built-in book-shelves and multiple fireplaces had presented a challenge, but she was pleased with the result.

"This took you two months?" Zebadiah was impressed with the result, the room practically glowed.

"Yes," she cleared her throat again, "the other rooms shouldn't take as long, there's not as much to do as there was in this one, and Thomas has ex-plained that some of the rooms on the third floor will remain painted." She did her best to hide her displeasure over this fact, but she failed miserably. For a supposed witch she was very easy to read.

Her eyes met his across the room as they assessed each other silently, and Zebadiah couldn't help but think that there was something familiar about her, as if he had met her somewhere before.

"Are you sure we haven't met before?" he asked suddenly, the feeling was too strong to ignore.

"I'm sure," she said, looking away from him.

He walked over to her, getting into her personal space, and he could hear her sharp intake of breath as his shoulder brushed hers, but she kept her eyes forward as if the light touch hadn't happened. "A lover's knot," he said, tracing the outline as she had. "I wonder what it means?"

"Probably that whoever built the house was in love," she said simply as she stepped away from him.

Zebadiah was intrigued, most woman in his circle pushed themselves into his space. It was as if he made her uneasy.

"Perhaps," he said before suddenly turning towards the others in the room. "What do you think of it Gianna?" he asked, watching the woman as she crossed the room when she was spoken to, wrapping her arm in his as she reached him, proving his point.

"It's lovely Zebadiah," she assured him in a purr.

"So lovely that I might have to reconsider leaving the paint in the other rooms, it seems a shame to put so much effort into only a few rooms." Zebadiah noted the excited spark in Lucy's eyes, and he paused as he realized how pleased he was that he had put it there.

He extracted his arm from Gianna's and held out his hand once more to Lucy, watching as she bit her lip in hesitation, but whatever she was thinking she pushed it aside as she placed her hand in his. He watched as her eyes dilated once more, but this time instead of growing pale she turned a pleasing shade of pink, and he couldn't help but wonder what she was thinking.

Realizing that he had been holding her hand longer than was acceptable for a polite handshake he dropped it, surprised that he was sorry to do so.

"It was a pleasure to meet you Lucy Monore," he said with a rare smile. Lucy looked up and met his eyes, and he swore he heard little girls giggling. The sound was so real that he looked at the other two women in the room to make sure it wasn't them.

When he looked back at Lucy she had turned away and moved back towards her tools, and he realized that the sound must have been his imagination.

With a farewell to Thomas, he motioned for the other ladies to proceed him and they left, but not before he took one last glance at the small woman with her ridged back.

Perhaps she was a witch because she had certainly bewitched him with only a handshake. He felt an intense need to know more about her, and he hadn't felt anything like it since he was a very young man. He would be lying to himself if he didn't acknowledge that it excited him.

Chapter 5

Lucy worked steadily for what little time was left in her day before she could head to the safety of her home to regroup. She had hoped that Thomas would return to tell her more about what had happened earlier, but he must have gotten held up somewhere because he never did.

As her little car pulled up at the end of the dock that lead to her grandmother's house, she gave a silent sigh of relief. Here was her normal, she knew that her grandmother had made them a delicious supper. They would eat and then she could spend the rest of the evening working on her grandmother's birthday present. It was an old ornate four poster bed frame that she had found in the attic. It had seen better days, but it had been in the family for years. She was going to restore it to its former glory and then buy her grandmother all new bedding, bedding fit for a queen. It was something her grandmother had told her she had wanted for a long time, and now she had the money to make it happen.

As Lucy got out of the car, Shy, their protector, came prancing down the dock towards her. It amazed her that, for such a bedraggled dog that had led a rough life in the few short years he had been on earth, he managed to carry himself with such assurance and swagger. So much in fact, one automatically thought he was larger than he was, and he reminded her a lot of Zebadiah in that sense. Shy also reminded her of Zebadiah because he didn't trust anyone, and she had a feeling that Zebadiah didn't trust many people either. However, despite his trust issues Shy had chosen Lucy and her grandmother, Etta, as his to protect, and she was glad that they had him, especially since their house was in the middle of nowhere.

Her grandmother's house looked old and dilapidated on the outside, like an old shack that sat over the water, but inside was an oasis of color and antiques that was welcoming and warm. Her grandmother had been born in the house and had lived there her entire life, and she wouldn't consider living anywhere else, although Lucy had tried to convince her to move to the city with her many times.

Lucy once again thought of Zebadiah as she started down the pier, pausing to look out over the still marsh water. The evening sounds of frogs and cicadas all faded, as did the gentle breeze that stirred the warm night air and moss hanging over head. She wasn't thinking of any one thing but all of it thrown together, his eyes, the feel of his hand, his smile. She frowned when she remembered the vision of breaking glass and seeing red, it wasn't good, but she didn't think that it was a given, only a warning; but of what she couldn't be sure.

"Baby Girl, why are you just standing there looking at nothing?" her grandmother asked from the doorway of their house.

"I met him today Etta," she said, not hearing the words as she said them, it was as if she was in some sort of trance.

"Yes, I know." Her grandmother walked up to her, placing her hand on her arm. "Come eat and tell me about it?"

The contact startled Lucy as she looked over at her grandmother's weathered face. "About what?"

"About him," she explained as she led the way into the house.

Lucy blushed, she had never really talked about boys or men with her grandmother before, or with anyone before, it was new territory. "How did you know?"

"You just told me," Lucy followed her into the house and moved to the kitchen in the back of the house to wash her hands. Then, still in a dream like stupor, she joined her grandmother at the table without paying any attention to the delicious meal spread there.

"So, tell me about him," the woman insisted. She was small like Lucy and her eyes were just a gray as was her hair. The only difference was her lined face.

"He was large, dark, and cold." Lucy shivered at the memory, astounded that such a man had her hypnotized.

"But?" the older woman asked as she watched the beautiful young woman in front of her eat absentmindedly.

"He smiled, he was told I was a witch, but he still treated me with respect."

"Who told him you were a witch?" Etta's voice was sharp, and Lucy only shrugged in response.

They sat in silence for a moment, both with their own thoughts.

"What did you see?" Etta finally asked her.

"I saw me," she said so softly that her grandmother had to strain to hear her.

The woman nodded as if that was expected. "And?"

"There were two little girls and he was happy."

"And you, were you happy?" Etta's eyes couldn't miss the glow that covered her granddaughter's face.

"Yes, I was, and I was pregnant." She nodded happily at the memory, as if assuring herself that she had it right in her head, but then she frowned as the other memory invaded her happy glow. "I also saw red." She knew it was a bad omen, and the frown on her grandmother's face proved that fact.

"Which vision came first?"

"The happy one." Lucy looked up at Etta, waiting for her to explain, and she was relieved when she saw her nod.

"That's good, it's a warning only, there is an evil that surrounds you both. You will have to be on your guard until it shows itself." Her grandmother leaned forward. "Was there anything else?"

Lucy blushed at the memory of the third vision. It was an intimate image of her and Zebadiah entwined in a large bed, she hadn't been able to see where one body started and the other one stopped.

Etta gave a knowing smile. "Keep that one to yourself," she chuckled, and Lucy's blush deepened. "What is his name?"

"Zeb, Zebadiah Abbott." Lucy let name roll off her tongue, it sounded so familiar now.

Etta was thoughtful for a moment, as if considering whether to tell her something or not. "When you were born your great aunt told your future and I always puzzled over it, but now it makes sense." Etta shook her head as she took a moment to remember her sister who had embraced their gifts and honed her skill, making it her life's work.

"Tell me?" Lucy begged, searching for something that would help it all make sense in her head.

"She said, 'Her life will be blessed, and she will be content when the name which begins with the ending and ends with the beginning arrives.' It's rather impressive," Etta said with a sad smile.

A sudden knock on the screen door startled them and Shy gave a little growl. The fact that he hadn't attacked the door could only mean that it was Thomas.

"Come in Thomas!" Etta called, moving to the kitchen to get another plate.

"Did you psychic abilities divine that it was me?" he joked as he entered the house, giving Shy a wide berth.

Etta laughed. "No, Shy did." She gave him a hug and he kissed her cheek before she handed him a plate. He was about to refuse when he saw what she had made.

"Only a little, Hope has dinner waiting," he said as he dished up and started to eat quickly.

"Then why are you here?" Lucy asked, watching him with amusement.

Lucy looked at her grandmother and they both agreed in an unspoken moment that they shouldn't tell Thomas as they gave him a few minutes to eat.

"I wanted to get your take on Abbott," he said with a full mouth.

"I hardly had a chance to judge," Lucy said offhandedly. "He sounded like he was reasonable, and he treated me with respect even after he was told I might be a witch."

"You're bound to like him because he's going to let you have your own way with the third floor." He grinned as he pushed his plate away, having finished eating in record time.

Lucy smiled and nodded. "I'll add that he is possibly a wise man."

"He makes me nervous. I would hate to cross him." Thomas looked up at Lucy. "Did he make you nervous?"

"No, I sense he is a fair man," Lucy said, knowing it was what he wanted to hear. "But I agree, I wouldn't cross him or mess with what is his. I have a feeling he doesn't easily forgive." She suppressed a shiver as she said it.

They spoke for a few more minutes before Thomas nodded as he stood, he had gotten what he wanted, an assurance that he wouldn't have any trouble with Zebadiah Abbott.

"You better head home before Hope sends out a search party," Lucy suggested then watched as he left as quickly as he had arrived.

She couldn't help but think that, while Thomas would have no trouble with Zebadiah, she would have a heap of it, along with a broken heart. Because even though her aunt had foretold it, and her own visions had confirmed it, she still had a hard time believing that a strong and powerful man like Zebadiah Abbott could love an outcast like herself.

"He's a strong man, he's up for the challenge," Etta said softly from the other side of the room.

Lucy didn't ask her how she knew what she was thinking, there were just some things that were better left unexplained.

Chapter 6

Lucy had the windows open and the warm breeze cooled her heated skin while the gentle night sounds soothed her. It was after dark and she was still steadily working on the last details of the woodwork in the study. If Thomas knew that she was working by herself in the house this late he would kill her. She had locked all the doors behind her and, unless a person was skilled in wall climbing, she was safe even with the windows open on the second story.

It was hot and since she was by herself she had lost her ballcap and dropped the top of her overalls so that the air could cool her core better. She would be happy when Thomas finally got the HVAC installed. She was kneeling in front of one of the glass fronted cabinets that covered one entire wall of the study, applying a final coat of stain, and she didn't hear the footsteps until they were in the room. Pausing, she took stock of her situation, trying not to panic. Whomever it was most likely had a key and hadn't yet bothered her. It was probably Thomas, and he would probably be angry.

Slowly, she eased herself out of the tight space, setting her brush to the side, before turning to look behind her.

It wasn't Thomas, it was Zebadiah Abbott, and he towered over her holding a very large box. He didn't look angry, he didn't really look as if he felt anything as his cold eyes took in her appearance, lingering on her silver hair.

She cleared her throat as she stood, not sure what she should say, or if she should say anything at all. In her experience it was always best to let the other person speak first.

"Isn't it a little late for you to still be working?" he asked as he set the box down. "I didn't approve overtime pay?"

"I don't get paid by the hour, I get paid by the job." She stood as still as a statue, watching him warily.

"Still, I can't imagine that it's safe for anyone to be working on a job site by themselves? I'll have to discuss this with Thomas." She noticed that his hand was clenching and unclenching, as if he was trying to expend his energy in that one movement as opposed to expressing it through a look or his voice.

"Thomas would agree with you, which is why he doesn't know I'm here."

He waited still not saying a word, and Lucy's usually strong resistance to pressure failed.

"I lost two days this week due to personal reasons, and sometimes it's easier to do the staining when the others aren't here. There is less dust in the air."

"But you have the windows open? And you still have plenty of time until this job is finished before you need to start pulling all-nighters." It was easy to tell that he would win this argument by simple logic.

"You're upset because I'm here." She nodded. She got it, she had wanted to be alone which is exactly why she was there as well. The only difference was that it was his house not hers and he had a right to be there

"No, I'm upset because it's not safe for you to be here on your own? Do you do this kind of thing regularly?"

She bit back a bitter smile. "I'm almost always on my own. The doors were locked so I'm as safe as I would be in my own house?"

"You live alone?" He was using logic again.

"No." She shook her head. Realizing that she wasn't going to win the argument, she looked down at her supplies. "Can I have half an hour to finish up here. Thomas mentioned that you wanted to start moving your things into this space, and I wanted to have it done sooner rather than later. If I can finish this up this evening, it will be all yours." She should have led with that and the thought must have shown on her face because she swore she saw a glimmer of amusement in his eyes, but it was gone so quickly she very well could have imagined it.

"Please, finish. If I continue to move boxes up here, will it stir up too much dust?" he asked, and this time Lucy's eyes sparked with amusement.

"Perhaps, but go ahead anyway." She nodded, turning back towards her work fighting a grin. She had a feeling they might share a similar sense of humor.

"I appreciate your permission," he said drily before he left the room, and as soon as he was gone Lucy didn't bother to hide her grin.

He hauled five large boxes up the stairs and he was even breathing heavily by the time he was done. He asked her which shelves he could use, and she told him, watching out of the corner of her eye as he started to unpack books and other items.

"So, your boyfriend, fiancé, or husband is alright with you working by yourself up here after dark?" He asked after a few minutes of silence.

"I don't have a boyfriend, fiancé, or husband to object," she said as she smoothed out a streak in the stain.

"Then who do you live with?" he asked absentmindedly, as if he was only trying to make conversation.

"My grandmother, and she doesn't mind either," Lucy assured him.

"Thomas-"

"Look, please don't tell him. I promise I won't do it again." She stopped what she was doing and turned to look at him.

He regarded her silently for a moment before nodding his consent, and they both went back to work. "If you do get behind and need to pull a late night let me know, I'm planning to spend more time here, and if I am here then there is no reason you couldn't do that."

His offer surprised her, and she turned to stare at him once again. He must have felt her gaze because he stopped what he was doing and looked over at her.

"I didn't expect that." She shook her head.

This time he did smile. "Neither did I."

Lucy returned his smile and looked away shyly as she remembered the vision she had had of them together.

A few moments later he stood and walked out onto the dark veranda that was at the opposite end of the room. The study was massive and ran the length of one side of the house. Lucy had felt the atmosphere between them change and she started to pack up, sensing he had had enough for one night.

She had packed her last tool when she once again heard footsteps behind her. Turning she saw Joel Bradley looking at he from the shadows. Not saying a word, Lucy continued to pack her things.

"Lucy, are you trespassing again?" he asked in his slow drawl.

"No Joel, I'm working. Thomas already explained this to you." She did her best to sound unconcerned.

"But it's after hours," he walked up to where she was kneeling down placing here things in her bag, "I'm sure that's not allowed." His manner was definitely aggressive as he lifted his toe up and sat it on the tool she had just reached for.

"I'm allowed to be here Joel," she said tugging on her tool, but he refused to move his foot as he knelt to her level. He reached out and swatted one of the shoulder straps for her overalls.

"Why are you only half-dressed Lucy, is that an invitation?" he reached up and tucked a piece of her hair behind her ear.

"Back off Joel!" she insisted as she yanked her tool out from under his foot and he fell backwards.

She watched as his face turned red and then purple in anger.

"Why you little witch!" he ground out, reaching for her arm and twisting it.

"Let me go!" she hissed, trying to jerk her arm free.

"Is there a problem here?" Zebadiah asked from the veranda's doorway.

Lucy closed her eyes in silent relief at the sound of his voice, she had forgotten he was there. When she finally chanced a look at him he was as still as stone and just as cold. His eyes were dark hard pools as he looked down on Joel.

Lucy watched as Joel jumped to his feet, looking from one to the other. "So, this is where you're bringing them?" he said, his voice full of contempt. "I should arrest both of you!"

"On what charges?" Zebadiah looked at him with a false calm, but Lucy noted his fist clenching and unclenching next to his leg.

"Solicitation!" he spat.

Lucy closed her eyes in mortification. Who knew what Zebadiah had thought of her before for this, but now...

"Stop it Joel! You know you're making that up!" she hissed.

"No, I don't know. Everyone knows about you Monroes, the apples don't fall very far from the tree." He grinned, thinking he finally had her.

She wanted the ground to open and swallow her.

"I don't know who you are or why you're here in my house, but I'm asking you to leave now," Zebadiah said calmly.

"Your house?" Joel asked, looking unsure as his gaze moved back to Lucy, who sat on the floor with her head bowed in embarrassment.

"Yes, my house. Lucy is working on the restoration of the woodwork, that's why she is here so late."

"You're Abbott?" Joel looked unsure.

"Yes, would you like to see some identification?" His voice had steel in it, as if daring him to ask for such a thing.

Joel must have finally picked up on his mistake because he swallowed then looked towards the door while the silence stretched on for what felt like forever.

"No, that won't be necessary, I saw a light and thought that someone might be trespassing, I only wanted to check and make sure everything was as it should be," he insisted as he moved towards the door. At the continued silence he nodded once more then left quickly, and Lucy listened to his fading footsteps, wishing she could make as quick a getaway as he had.

"How long has that been going on?" Zebadiah asked, walking to the window, watching what Lucy could only guess was Joel leaving the property.

Lucy shrugged, not wanting to go into the details. There was no point, it wasn't as if it was going to stop anytime soon. She packed up the last of her tools then adjusted her overalls before reaching for her ballcap and pushing it onto her head.

"I'm sorry," she stood, "I'll get out of your way now." She started for the door but halfway there she felt his hand on her arm, stopping her, and her eyes closed at the sensation of fire that coursed though her veins at his touch.

"How long has that been going on?" he asked once again.

"My entire life in one form or another." She moved away from his warm touch, a touch that she wanted to move towards not away from. "I think I'll take your advice and only work on the site during regular hours from now on." She nodded and started down the stairs and he followed behind her.

"I can see myself out," she insisted.

"I'm sure you can, but I want to make sure you make it to your car safely. You are on my property after all, and I would be responsible if anything happened to you." He followed her out to the car and waited while she stored her stuff.

Lucy couldn't help but compare her little car to his very expensive one, and he stood back as she slammed her door and rolled down the window.

"Thanks for the save," she said once more before she started the engine.

He looked as if he wanted to say something, but he must have changed his mind because he stepped away from the car and started back towards the house without a backwards glance.

Feeling sorrier for herself than she had in a long time, Lucy started the short drive home, wondering what Zebadiah thought of her after that little encounter. With her bad luck, he probably believed every word and would treat her the same as everyone else in town did from now on, like an outcast.

Chapter 7

In the weeks that followed Zebadiah spent more time at the house, and Lucy had done her best to avoid him as much as possible. When their paths did cross they were polite to each other and not a word was mentioned about their encounter with Joel.

Zebadiah had moved completely into the study, even to the point of putting a bed at the end of the room near the balcony doors. Lucy had only needed to enter the room once or twice since her last encounter with him, but she could feel his presence even when he wasn't there, and she loved the way the restored room look lived in. It was as if it had become the heart of the house, feeding off the energy Zebadiah left behind. Everything on the job was going smoothly and progressing at a rapid pace. The house was happy and that made Lucy happy.

She had moved down to the first floor to work on the drawing room. It was a large beautiful room that was filled with amazing details. The ceiling had wood paneling as did the walls, and she had never seen carvings as ornate as those that graced the mantle and fireplace surround. The room would be just as impressive as the study when she was finished with it.

Thomas had told her that the fireplace was going to need a liner installed to make it operable, and she was pleased that Zebadiah was going to make it functional once again. It would be wonderful to have roaring fire in the room on a really cold night in the winter. She was smiling at the thought, as if she was sharing the house's joy, when she heard a noise behind her.

Turning she saw a very little girl of about four years watching her through bangs that were a little too long.

"Hello," she greeted, Lucy's smile growing at her cute little face. Her hair and eyes were dark, and she looked naturally reserved, so when she smiled back Lucy felt as if she had achieved something important. "Who are you?" Lucy asked setting her brush off to one side.

"Eden!" She watched as a woman with equally dark hair and eyes caught the little girl by the hand. "You shouldn't wander off because the house isn't safe." The woman glanced up at Lucy and gave her a vague smile. "I'm looking for my brother, Zebadiah?" she asked.

"I haven't seen him yet this morning, but if he's here he'll be in the study on the second floor," Lucy supplied as she watched Gianna Beckett join the woman and little girl.

Gianna took her time looking around the room, assessing the work, before her gaze landed on Lucy with apparent disgust. She didn't try to introduce Lucy and the woman.

"Gianna, would you stay here and keep an eye on Eden? I want to talk to Zebadiah alone." The woman didn't wait for an answer as she started up the steps in the hallway.

Eden didn't seem to be troubled by the development, and she kept her eyes glued to Lucy while Gianna looked almost afraid at the prospect of being left alone with the little girl. Amused, Lucy turned back towards her work, picking up her brush.

A few moments later Eden was standing next to her. "What are you doing?" she whispered.

"I'm dusting, would you like to try?" Lucy asked just as softly.

Eden looked over her shoulder at Gianna who was busy doing something on her phone and not paying her any attention. With a nod, the little girl knelt, taking the brush from Lucy. It looked abnormally large in her little hand. "I'm Eden. What do I do?"

"I'm Lucy, and you pretend like you're painting and get all of the dust and crumbs out of the cabinet."

Lucy watched as the young girl leaned in and gave the cabinet a few gentle swipes. "Perfect, but don't be afraid to get in those corners." She reached into her bag and took out a small dental scraper, it was perfect for the detail work, and began to work at the paint around the flower motifs on the mantle. When Eden finished the first cabinet, Lucy opened the next one and let her start again. Lucy had already cleaned them once, so it was an easy job for the little girl and there was nothing that could harm her.

"What are you doing!" Gianna suddenly shrieked at the young girl.

Eden was so content in her job that she either didn't hear Gianna or she thought she was talking to someone else, and Lucy watched as she stormed towards the little girl and pulled her out of the cabinet.

They didn't hear Zebadiah or his sister as they entered the room.

"I'm dusting!" Eden held up her brush wiping it in Gianna's face, making her even more angry.

"Stay away from her, she isn't safe!" Gianna hissed, pulling the little girl even further away from Lucy.

"You're hurting me, and I was working!" The little voice sounded so grown up that Lucy turned away as she bit back a smile. When she looked up she caught Zebadiah's cold gaze on her and her smile faded. When she glanced over at his sister she looked as amused by her daughter's explanation as Lucy had been.

"What are you working at?" The dark-haired woman asked.

"Lucy needed my help dusting the cabinet." She waved the brush again.

"I did, and you did an excellent job. Why don't you close that cabinet so that I know it's already been done," she suggested and watched the little girl do as she was asked.

"Eden, why don't you join me over here, darling," Gianna cooed.

Eden's little head tilted at the strange endearment coming from her lips, it was a dead giveaway that she had never been so sweet to the little girl before.

"I told you I'm working," she insisted once again, moving to stand beside Lucy.

"Sweetie, Lucy isn't..." Lucy waited for Gianna to finish that statement and Zebadiah did as well as Lucy noted his hand start pulsing next to his leg.

"It's fine Eden. It is just about lunch time anyway, and I never miss my lunch," Lucy looked down at her with a sweet smile and had to push away the temptation to smooth her bangs back out of her eyes.

Eden thought about it for awhile then looked up at Lucy. "Can I keep the brush?" she asked in a whisper.

"Eden," her mother warned at her rudeness.

"Of course, you can help your mother dust at home." Lucy said without a second thought about how expensive the brush was. With what Zebadiah was paying her she could afford to buy a new one. "But you take very good care of it, it's mighty expensive," she warned in a whisper.

"I will," she assured Lucy in a whisper before she danced over to her mother.

"Lucy Monroe, this is my sister Zelda Abbott, Zelda this is Lucy, she's restoring all of the wood work in the house." Zebadiah introduced them.

Zelda walked towards her and held out her hand. "It's nice to meet you Lucy. Thank you for entertaining Eden for me." Lucy took her hand, but dropped it quickly.

"I enjoyed it just as much as she did, it's always nice to make a new friend." Lucy smiled over at Eden who grinned back, happy to be called a friend.

"We won't keep you from your lunch Lucy," Zebadiah said, dismissing her.

Lucy nodded and reached down grabbing the bag which held her lunch before she walked towards them. She had to squeeze past Zebadiah to get through the doorway, and she couldn't help but breathe a little deeper as she inhaled his clean scent.

"Don't forget to show Eden the attic if you get the chance," Lucy winked at the girl. "There's plenty up there for her to investigate." When she looked up it was directly in to Zebadiah's black eyes, and for a moment everything stood still, and she swore she felt his hand caress her arm, but when she looked down both hands were firmly at his sides, and one of them continued to clench and unclench as he waited for her to leave them.

The touch had felt so real that there could have been no way she could have imagined it, but he hadn't touched her. Had he been thinking about it? Had their minds been so attuned that it was as if he had touched her without really doing so?

Shaking off the odd notion, she forced herself to say goodbye to Eden one last time before she moved out of the house and down the front steps. There was a tree near the river and she would enjoy her lunch under its shady branches.

As she settled in she had to wonder; if an imagined touch had sent such shock waves through her what would his actual touch feel like?

She was upset that he might be displeased with her interactions with Eden. In the future, perhaps she should do her best to avoid the girl. She would hate to upset Eden or get her in trouble.

She gave a sad sigh, so it went, another person who wasn't willing to give her a chance, who believed the rumors. She had hoped he would be different, that her dream would come true, but it seemed highly unlikely with the way things were going.

Chapter 8

Zebadiah had taken the time to show his sister around the house with Gianna following their every step. He had arranged for his sister to come and see the house a few days earlier, and he had not been pleased that she had invited Gianna along for the ride.

Gianna was one of the reasons he was spending more time in Belfort, she kept appearing at places in town that he frequented, restaurants, the gym, and even events that were invitation only. She was becoming a problem that he would have to quickly deal with, and his sister's constant attempts to throw them together weren't helping. First, she had hung on to his realtor, invading that meeting, then she had tagged along with his sister after convincing her that there was an unspoken agreement that he would be taking her to the Annual Abbott Gala. He had set his sister straight on the matter during her visit, and he hoped that little scene with Gianna and Lucy in the drawing room had cleared up any doubt Zelda may have had on the subject.

But he realized that he still had to get the message that he wasn't available across to Gianna, and he believed he had figured out a way to do that. A way which might mean that he would get to spend a little more time with Lucy Monroe, if she agreed to his plan.

He wandered into the drawing room from the veranda and saw Lucy as she busily scraped way at something on the mantel. Taking his time, he slowly entered the room, watching her small form as her head tilted one way and then the other as she assessed her work.

Suddenly, as if she sensed his presence, she spun around and looked at him, her eyes wide in concern. "I'm sorry, did you want to use the room again?" she asked as her eyes darted behind him to see who was following.

"No, my company has left. I would have invited you to join us, but I didn't think you would feel comfortable around Gianna." He walked further into the room, moving to stand behind her to see what she was doing. He couldn't help but reach out and run a finger over the fresh wood that she had exposed.

"It will be just as lovely as the study when it's finished."

He could hear the pleasure that the thought brought her. "You enjoy what you do?" he asked, looking down at her. She was so small and delicate, and he felt an overwhelming urge to protect her.

"I love it, I love bring new life back to forgotten things. I love to see them loved once more."

"Like this house?" he asked, looking around the large room. "How will you tackle the ceiling?" He looked up, the idea of it seemed daunting to him.

"Thomas will set up some scaffolding for me." She pulled out a brush from her back pocket and brushed away some dust from the mantel, and he had the impression that he was making her nervous.

"You were right about taking Eden up to the attic, how did you know all of the stuff was up there?" he asked, wanting to put her at ease by talking about something trivial, but it was the wrong thing to say because she tensed at the question.

"Thomas and I used to play up there as children. We used to play all over this house and the grounds. Most people were to afraid to come here, so it was our own little escape from everyone else. I'm glad that she liked it, she seems like a sweet little girl."

"She is sweet and a little too spunky at times.' He responded automatically while he thought about her and Thomas's true relationship. They appeared to be unusually close, but he knew that Thomas was married with a child on the way. Were they past lovers or were they still having an affair? The idea of it made him angry, but he was afraid to look to deeply into the reason why, and since it wasn't his business he didn't ask any questions.

As if conjured up by his thoughts, Thomas appeared in the doorway, looking from one to the other.

"Lucy, Don Mankin is about ten minutes out," he informed her gently, before he looked between them once more and left.

Zebadiah watched as she started to pack up her tools quickly. "Are you going somewhere?"

"I'll be back in a few hours," she said as she picked up her bag and swung it over her shoulder, looking around her to make sure that she had picked up everything.

"Where are you going?" he asked. He found the entire interaction odd.

"Just up the road for a little bit," she said, walking towards the back of the house where the crew parked their cars.

"Can you give me a few more moments of your time before you leave, I have a favor to ask of you?" he blocked her path, and she looked desperate to be gone.

"No, I can't," she shook her head pushing past him. The brush of her body against his was electric, and once again he had to fight himself from reaching out and touching her. He had wanted to earlier and had barely been able to control himself.

"I insist, I only need a few minutes of your time." He heard his voice turned hard, he wasn't going to take no for an answer. He knew he was going about it all wrong, but for the first time in his life he felt out of his element.

"I really can't stay," She moved away from him once more, and this time he did reach out and stop her by placing his hand on her arm.

"Why?"

"You're living here, but to do that legally you need a Certificate of Occupancy and Don Mankin is the county building inspector, he is coming here to issue it," she explained as she looked anxiously over her shoulder.

"What does that have to do with you?" He really was confused.

She looked as if she wasn't going to answer, but as she heard voices in the other room she said quickly, "He won't step foot in the house if I'm here." Then she wrenched her arm from his hand and darted down the back-veranda steps and towards her car.

He watched as she climbed into the car and started it then drove away. He found himself very angry all the sudden, and he forced himself to push the feeling back, finding the cold calm that had taken years to develop, managing to do so just as Thomas entered with a very tall and skinny man with greying hair. Thomas's eyes darted around the room making sure it was all clear before he sagged with obvious relief.

"Do you mind if I tag along?" Zebadiah asked, keeping his face carefully neutral.

Thomas took a moment to introduce the two men then the tour began, and Zebadiah was careful to keep an eye on both men, watching how they interacted with each other. One thing he had learned over the years was that you needed to take the time to learn the players, that way their weaknesses were easier to spot, which in turn made it easier for him to get his own way in the end, and he always got his own way in the end.

He just wasn't sure what exactly it was that he wanted yet, but he had a feeling it had something to do with Lucy Monroe because she seemed to take up more of his thoughts lately, more than she should.

Chapter 9

Lucy walked into the quiet sanctuary of the church, finding a pew in the back, she sank into it as she let the cold air from the HVAC wash over her. She had to admit to herself that she was shaken from Zebadiah's intensity, he had been determined that she stay. When he had blocked her and she had been forced to squeeze by him, it had felt so much like an embrace, and when he had reached out to stop her, all she had wanted to do was stay. However, she knew that if she had stayed Thomas would have failed inspection.

Closing her eyes, she took a deep breath in an attempt to settle herself, she couldn't help but wonder what Zebadiah had wanted to ask her. What possible favor could he want from her, and why was it so urgent?

"Lucy?" Thomas's father, Fred Kane, joined her.

"Hello Mr. Kane. Thanks for unlocking the church for me." She looked over at him with a smile and he returned it as he sat next to her.

"I was happy to, I don't get to see you all that often anymore." He took her hand in his and patted it.

"I know, I try to keep a low profile, and Thomas has a lot going on right now." She took off her ballcap and sat it on the pew next to her.

"But he should always have time for his friends," the older man insisted. He looked so much like Thomas that it was uncanny sometimes.

"He does, and he is always there when I need him," she defended.

"You should have been at the wedding last year." It was evident that he still hadn't let that one go yet.

"I was invited and Thomas insisted that I come, but it is the bride's day, and Hope didn't want me there, and I love Thomas enough not to make his wife miserable." She rested her head on the older man's shoulder.

He had been like a father to her over the years. Thomas had gotten his father's tender and accepting heart.

"There was a time that I thought the two of you would grow up to get married." He smiled fondly at the memory.

"Nah, we're to much like brother and sister for that to ever happen. Besides, he took one look at Hope and was head over heels in love." Lucy couldn't quite keep the wistfulness out of her voice.

"Why don't you start coming to church Lucy? I would love to have you here on Sundays." He had been issuing the same invitation since she was a girl, and she had been turning it down just as long.

"Maybe, we'll see." The fact of the matter was no one wanted her there. They all wanted to believe that they were good accepting Christian's and every Sunday at church was their time to do that. If she started to attend they would be reminded that they weren't as accepting as they should be. She didn't doubt that most of them would accept her at a Sunday service without a word spoken, but there would be those like Don Mankin that would demand that she be blocked from entering the building.

They talked for quite some time, reminiscing about her and Thomas's youth and talking about the LeClair mansion before he rose to leave.

"I just got back from my daily visit to the hospital and was going to fix me a late lunch, would you care to join me?" he asked, patting her hand once more.

Lucy shook her head. "No, thank you. I have a lot on my mind, do you mind if I just sit here silently for a bit?" she asked.

"Not at all, you know where the key is, lock up behind you." He dropped a kiss on her hair, and Lucy noticed he paused as he looked towards the back of the church.

"Hello," he greeted, "can I help you?" he asked with his usual welcoming smile.

Lucy froze, upset that her peace had been disrupted and now she would have to find somewhere else to wait, she reached over for her ballcap and put it back on her head.

"I wanted to talk to Lucy," Zebadiah's deep voice responded.

"Lucy?" Fred asked her.

Lucy sat up and looked over her shoulder. "Zebadiah Abbott meet Fred Kane, Fred is Thomas's father, Mr. Abbott owns the LeClair mansion." Lucy introduced the two then sat back against the pew and listened as they had a brief friendly conversation about the weather and the mansion before Fred left them.

"Please Lucy, call me Zebadiah," he insisted as he sat next to her on the pew. He was entirely too close for comfort and she could feel the heat as it radiated off his body, especially where his leg and shoulder brushed up against hers.

She nodded, still not saying anything but agreeing to his request. "Why are you here, and how did you know where to find me?"

"Thomas told me, I let him know that I had a favor to ask you, and he sent me to let you know that Don Mankin has left the property."

"A text would have done fine," she insisted.

"Yes, it would have, but as I said I wanted to talk to you, and I didn't want you to get away again." Zebadiah looked around the small church. "Do you attend church here?" he asked, taking his time in getting to the point.

"No," she responded, keeping it simple. She reached up and tucked a piece of hair under her hat.

"Why do you wear the hat all of the time?" he asked looking down at her.

Lucy could feel his eyes on her, but she refused to look up at him. "My hair makes people uncomfortable," she supplied.

"Then why don't you let it go back to its natural color?"

"This is its natural color, and before you suggest I dye it, I used to, but it was too expensive to maintain, and the town would only think I was trying to hide something." She shrugged as she remembered how she had thought it would make a difference when she was younger. The hat seemed the best comprise.

"Did you get your C/O?" she asked, changing the subject.

"Yes," his response was curt, as if he wasn't pleased by the fact, or maybe it was her asking the question that displeased him.

"You wanted to ask me for a favor?" she asked, in an attempt to direct him towards his reason for being there so that she could make her escape. His nearness unsettled her.

He nodded and shifted his body so that he could look at her. "I need a date."

"And your first choice is me?" she asked, her disbelief obvious.

"Yes, it is my company's non-profit's annual gala. We host it every year, this year the theme is black and white."

"And you thought my hair would be a good match?" she smiled at the little joke.

"I hadn't thought about it." His serious reply left her with little doubt the he hadn't thought about it.

"Won't Gianna mind?" she asked.

"Don't worry about Gianna," he insisted with such coldness that she would hate to be in that poor girl's shoes, she must have done something to make him mad.

"A lover's tiff?" Lucy asked off-handedly, there was no way she could seriously consider the offer.

"No, she disrespected you in my house," he responded in a hard voice.

"So, you pity me and are going to use me to prove a point and upset your girlfriend?" Lucy fired back, suddenly angry. She stood, but he grabbed her arm and pulled her back into the pew.

"No, I don't pity you. If you must know the truth, Gianna is proving to be a nuisance that I would rather not have in my life. I am asking you to attend the gala with me in an attempt to drive into her brain that my interests lay elsewhere," he said softly.

"Do they, lay elsewhere?" Lucy asked.

Zebadiah grinned and laughed aloud, and Lucy felt the gentle rumble of it all the way to her toes.

"Possibly, but either way, I get the feeling that you're not borderline psychotic," he said with an amused smile.

"No, but you should probably stay away from me just the same," she said sadly as she thought of all the grief that she had brought Thomas over the past years. "Besides, I don't have anything to wear to a gala." She stood and this time he let her.

"I'll be the judge of who I want to spend time with, but I thank you for the advice, and I will take care of the dress." He watched her as she watched him, they were both trying to figure out what the other one was thinking.

She really wanted to go, but did she dare?

"It's this Saturday in New Orleans, we will leave from here and return here, I promise to be a perfect gentleman, but I can't promise to have you home by midnight."

Lucy knew that it wasn't just about a date for her, it also meant going into a crowded room with a lot of people, and it would inevitably leave her ill, her senses overwhelmed when she saw visions of the choices that people made and where it would lead them. Parties, where the alcohol flowed freely, were the worst because people made very bad decisions.

But he couldn't know exactly what he had asked of her, and she really did want to go, maybe she could keep her eyes down and make sure she didn't talk or look at anyone.

Yeah, she would make a wonderful date. She shook her head once more. "There are more reasons-"

"Please," he asked simply.

Lucy didn't think he ever begged anyone for anything, so why was he begging her? It must be important, and she knew the moment she looked into his dark eyes that she had caved.

"Fine, but when it goes horribly wrong; I will be the first one to say I told you so," she insisted.

"I'm very rarely wrong Lucy, I feel that that is something that you should know about me." He stood and followed her out of the church, watching her as she locked the door.

"I'll let you know more later this week," he assured her as he got in his car, and she watched as he drove in the opposite direction of the house.

Lucy had the impression that he had already forgotten their conversation as he moved on to the next challenge of the day, whatever that might be.

Chapter 10

L ucy pulled around and parked at the back of the house. Zebadiah had left a short note for her the day after their conversation that told her that she should be at his house at three o'clock the following day. As she got out of her car she recognized his car but there was another behind it that she didn't recognize.

Letting herself into the house, she quietly listened before she started up the stairs. She could hear a gentle murmur of voices but she couldn't make out the words, and when she rounded the banister her eyes immediately connected with Zebadiah's, and she had the sudden vision of red once more. Was it another warning?

"Lucy," he greeted without smiling, although he did stand. "This is my personal assistant Summer, she is here to help you get ready for the party this evening." He motioned for her to enter the study.

As Lucy entered, her eyes landed on a young lady about her age. She was well rounded and had lots of corkscrew curls in light blond that covered her head. She was wearing a delicate dusting of makeup and her clothes were perfect for her. She was obviously in good hands when it came to fashion.

"Hi Lucy," she greeted with her hand out as she stood. "I hope your ready to play dress up? Zebadiah gave me an approximation of your size and I brought a few things for you to try."

Lucy blushed a little, embarrassed by the fact that she had been a topic of discussion for someone she hardly knew. She couldn't help but wonder what else Zebadiah had told her.

"Just remember that we need to leave by half past six," he reminded Summer as he waved them away and turned towards his computer.

Summer took her arm and pulled her across the hall to one of the unfinished rooms there. In it was a rack of clothing, boxes of shoes, and a table full of make-up and hair products. "Full makeover," she said with obvious glee. "It is times like these that I enjoy my job." She sighed as she walked around Lucy, taking in her size and appearance.

"Times like these?" Lucy asked, trying not to flinch as Summer reached up and took off her ballcap.

"Ummm, yes, when Zebadiah asks me to do something unusual, out of the norm, although he has never had me makeover one of his lady friends before."

Lucy didn't think she meant to be thoughtless with her comment, but she couldn't help cringe at the description. "I'm not one of his lady friends, I work for him just like you do," she insisted as she was pushed into a chair.

"What do you do for him?" Summer asked as she distractedly ran her hand through Lucy's hair. "Can I cut this?" she asked. "This is your natural color isn't it?" she asked in the next breath.

"Yes, and I restore furniture, I'm working on the house."

Summer nodded at her explanation, not really caring. "It's amazing that your hair and eyes are so light, but your brows and lashes are so dark." She grinned. "I have just the dress, I know it is a black and white ball, but when I was told about your coloring I snuck one in that will make a statement."

"I don't want to make a statement," Lucy declined the offer.

"You are Zebadiah Abbott's date for the evening, you need to make a statement, I have a feeling that was why he chose you in the first place, you're so lovely you'll be hard to miss." Summer walked over to the rack of clothes and sorted through it until she found what she wanted.

"Here, try this." She handed the dress to Lucy who took it. It was silver silk and it flowed through her hands like water. It was long with a high slit up one leg and hugged the body. It was sleeveless, and the neck dipped into a deep drape, there was no back.

"I can't wear this, what about underwear?" she asked, shocked by the idea of not wearing any.

"Don't worry, I have it covered, trust me." Summer pushed her back into the chair and turned her this way and that before picking up her scissors.

Lucy placed her hand on hers, stopping her. "Are you trained?"

"Yes, I was a hairstylist in my former life. Trust me, Zebadiah does," she insisted.

With a deep breath Lucy gave herself over to Summer.

The next three hours where a whirlwind of hair, makeup, and clothing with Summer talking a mile a minute. Telling Lucy all about herself and how Zebadiah had given her a chance when no one else would. That little fact made Lucy's heart beat a little faster as she hoped he might do the same for her.

There really wasn't any underwear to speak of, Summer had some large stickers that acted as a bra and the underwear was barely there, but as she slid the dress over Lucy's head and the silk caressed her skin, Lucy realized that there was no other choice because the dress hugged her so tightly.

Summer stepped back and looked at her with a grin. "My work here is done."

There was no mirror for Lucy to see herself in, so she had no clue if she looked like a clown or not.

"Take that Gianna!" Summer nodded and when Lucy looked over at her she blushed. "Sorry, but I don't like her, and I'm glad that Zebadiah isn't taking her seriously. I hope she will get the point this evening and leave him alone. She's been stalking him since Christmas."

That explained why Zebadiah was so insistent that she attend the gala as his date. He had hinted at it in the church but she hadn't been sure she had understood him or just how desperate he really was to get the point across to the woman.

"Hopefully, there will be a few other women that will be there that will also get the point. You're stunning so they should." Summer walked towards the door. "I'll be right back," she said as she slipped out of the room.

Lucy closed her eyes as she tried to erase the disappointment she felt at Summer's words. She had been in denial, but she had known what this date was all about because Zebadiah had explained it to her, but it hurt to hear the truth spoken by someone else.

Summer reappeared, pushing a floor length mirror that was on wheels with her. Lucy had noted it in the study but hadn't realized it was on wheels. Summer laughed at her stunned expression.

"Don't worry, he's not an overly vain man, but he does appreciate a custom-made suit and his tailor makes house calls," she explained as she wheeled the mirror to face Lucy.

Lucy turned to look at herself and couldn't hide her shock. "Summer!" She didn't recognize the woman who looked back at her. The dress was beautiful, she had felt exposed in it, but she needn't have worried. The silver dress coupled with her hair and her eyes made a dramatic statement. Her hair had been cut shorter and made her cheekbones and neck look delicate. She blinked back tears as she turned to Summer. "Thank you, but how can you be so sure this won't put ideas into my head about Zebadiah?" she joked.

Summer shook her head, turning serious. "You're a realist like me, you live in the here and now, not some vague future dream."

If only Summer realized exactly how hard Lucy fought to not do that very thing every time she saw Zebadiah.

"But I bet Zebadiah will have a few dreams of his own once he sees you," she crowed, proud of her work, and Lucy couldn't control her blush.

"You've never once thought about him like that?" Lucy couldn't help but ask, jealous at the thought.

"No, he's like a brother." Summer shook her head. Lucy got that because that was how she felt about Thomas. "Shall we do the big reveal now?" she asked, handing her a pair of silver heels, a cashmere shawl, and a little clutch bag. "You probably won't need the shawl, but it's better to have it and not need it."

Lucy looked at herself once more as she slipped on the shoes before she braced herself to follow Summer across the hall.

When they entered the study, Zebadiah had his back to them as he looked out the window while talking on his phone and she and Summer waited patiently until he was finished. Lucy couldn't help but admire the way his broad shoulders filled out his crisp white shirt.

When he turned towards them he was frowning but as he caught sight of Lucy his frown changed to a look of surprise. He let his gaze wander from the tips of her toes to the top of his head, taking his time, and Lucy felt as if he had physically touched her.

"Worth the wait I hope?" Summer asked as she looked between the two of them.

"Definitely, you look beautiful Lucy, and well worth being fashionably late."

As he reached for his tux jacket and threw it on then adjusted his cuffs, Lucy looked at the clock, noting that it was almost half past seven.

"I didn't realize that we had taken so long," Lucy said, surprised that they had.

"Summer knew exactly how long you were taking," Zebadiah teased as he walked around the desk. "Thank you, Summer. Why don't you leave with us and I'll lock up as we go?"

Summer nodded and went across the hall to gather her things while Zebadiah looked Lucy over once more. "You truly do look stunning," he complimented her.

Lucy thanked him nicely as Summer returned and he motioned towards the door for them to proceed him.

As Lucy passed him he placed his hand in the small of her bare back and she felt as if he had branded her. Everyone of her senses tuned into that one place and she closed her eyes at the sensation, tripping over her own feet in the process.

When Zebadiah's arms caught her around the waist and pulled her to him, it didn't make it any better, and as she looked up her eyes caught Summer's and she gave her knowing grin.

"I hope you two have fun tonight," she said as she darted ahead and down the stairs while Zebadiah gave Lucy time to regain her composure.

"Sorry, I'm not used to heels," she supplied, clearing her throat nervously while he still held her close. His hand was on her stomach and she could feel the muscles spasm at his touch. The warm silk between their skin heightened the sensation. His other hand came to rest on her hip and she had to close her eyes at the intimacy of it. It was as if he was touching her bare skin.

Lucy had the sudden suspicion that Summer had chosen the silk dress for that reason alone.

"I'm fine now." She cleared her throat and was sad to feel his hand drop away as he released her.

"Good, why don't you take my arm?" He held it out and she placed her hand in the crook of his elbow.

There were no more mishaps as they made their way to the party, and Lucy couldn't decide if she was disappointed or relieved.

Chapter 11

When they had arrived at the hotel, in the heart of the New Orleans' French Quarter, the party was in full swing. Zebadiah came around to pass his car keys off to the valet and help Lucy out of the car, and as she stepped out on to the pavement there were a few flashes from photographers. She hadn't thought about publicity. Zebadiah gave her little time to worry about it as he put his arm around her waist and she forgot about everything but his touch.

They entered the hotel and he instantly had people approach him who wanted to introduce people and be introduced. He turned to Lucy and she gave a quick shake of her head as he tried to pull her forward to introduce her.

"Don't you want to be introduced?" he asked softly in her ear so that only she could hear.

"No, I would rather remain a mystery, please." Her silver eyes meet his dark ones, and he considered her request for a moment before giving a nod of agreement.

Lucy did her best to avoid eye contact as she looked over at the dancers on the floor and then at the décor. It was a beautiful setting and if there hadn't been so many people there she probably would have enjoyed herself, but as it stood now, all she could see was a mass of people threating her peace of mind.

She should have said no, she shouldn't have come.

As if sensing her unease, Zebadiah pulled her close and wrapped his arm around her, resting his hand on her hip once more as her entire body rested against his. In that moment, she once again forgot about everything but him, she could feel his strong and steady heartbeat and she concentrated on that, letting his conversations wash over her as they moved around the room, oblivious to the impact she was making on the room, but she wasn't oblivious to the envious looks she was getting from the women.

****

Zebadiah wasn't oblivious to the attention Lucy was getting, he had been right, she was a perfect distraction. Her silver hair and eyes were captivating, and no one could take their eyes off her, least of all him. He couldn't help but think that she fit perfectly against him as he continued to hold her close as he worked the room, enjoying the way the silk of her dress felt as it slid across her skin.

When they sat down to dinner she only spoke when spoken to and kept her head down, as if she was afraid to talk to anyone, she hadn't struck him as someone who lacked confidence.

Eventually, he had to leave her for a moment to handle some business that he knew would need to be dealt, with and he watched as she nodded and walked away from him towards the bar. For some reason he wanted to chase after her, pull her back, and protect her, but he wasn't sure what he needed to protect her from.

******

Lucy walked towards the bar, keeping her head down and not meeting anyone's eyes, although she swore everyone's eyes were on her. When she reached the bar, she recognized the man behind it, he was from Belfort. Todd Rivers had never had much to say to her when they had gone to school together, so she wasn't sure what kind of reception she was going to get.

He paused when he saw her, looking around as if there would be more people from Belfort with her. The man he was serving at the other end of the bar said something and caught his attention once more, and Todd turned to him and finished serving him before he approached Lucy.

"Well Well, if it isn't little Lucy Monroe, the witch. How did you get an invite to this shindig?" He looked her over and she couldn't help but note the appreciation in his gaze "You clean up well, I'll give you that."

"May I have a white wine please?" she asked, as a man came to stand next to her at the bar. She moved a little away from him, immediately sensing something off about him.

"May I see your invitation?" he asked. It had been clear that the man he had just served hadn't provided an invitation, so she was confused as to why she needed to, and she said as much.

"I know him," he shrugged.

"You know me," she insisted.

"Yes, I do. Tell me what, or should I say who, are you doing to get into this party?"

The man next to her reached out and brushed an arm against hers as he reached for a piece of fruit on the bar. Lucy felt herself choke on the evil that rolled off him. She had only ever felt that kind of evil once, and it had been when her mother had brought home a boyfriend who had tried to hurt both her and her mother.

Lucy knew what was coming and she closed her eyes as a wave of nausea filled her. She saw him putting something in a drink, then lifting a body and walking into the darkness. She forced herself to look at him and follow his gaze, noting that it had landed on one of the waitresses.

Lucy moved to the other end of the bar and motioned for Todd to follow her, she knew it was hopeless, but she had to try. "That man, keep an eye on him, and don't let your waitresses leave on their own this evening," she begged.

"Why, is he your date?" Todd looked back over at the man. "Really Lucy, in that getup you could do better."

"Please Todd, he's not a nice man," she whispered, reaching for his arm.

"Don't touch me," he hissed, pulling his arm away as if she was diseased, then he motioned for one of the security men who then approached the bar.

"This woman doesn't have an invitation, would you please escort her off of the premises, she's harassing the guests," he insisted.

But Todd wasn't in Belfort any longer, not everyone here hated her, and some people were aware of what was going on around them. It also didn't hurt that she was a personal guest of Zebadiah's

"Miss Monroe is there a problem?" the security guard asked her, as he said something softly into his walkie-talkie.

Lucy didn't know what to do, she wished Zebadiah was here. She had the feeling that if she told him he would believe her. "I would like a white wine please," she requested softly.

"Please get Miss Monroe a white wine?" The security guard turned back to Todd, his face a blank mask.

Todd looked back and forth between the two, about to object, when Zebadiah joined them, placing his arm around Lucy in a protective manner.

"Is everything alright Lucy?" he asked. When her eyes met his he must have noted something in them because he pulled her aside. "What is it?"

"That man at the bar..."

"The bartender?" he asked, then waited patiently for her to respond as she tried to gain control of herself.

"No, the man sitting at the bar. He's evil, he is going to drug someone," she choked out between dry lips.

"Your wine," the guard said as he handed it to her.

She must have looked like she needed it, and she gave him a weak smile in response as Zebadiah looked over his shoulder at the man they were talking about.

"Did you see the drugs?"

"Not exactly, but he keeps looking at the waitresses as they pass by and I'm afraid..."

Zebadiah looked at her, his face a mask. "And the bartender?"

"Someone from Belfort," she shook her head as if he didn't matter, and he didn't, but the man at the bar did. "Please Zeb, I know it sounds strange, but please believe me. Can you just have someone keep an eye on him?" She hadn't realized she had called him Zeb as her eyes met his.

Zebadiah motioned for the security guard to join them and he was by their side in an instant.

"What happened with the bartender?" he asked.

"Please Zeb, it's not important."

"He called her a witch, refused to serve her, and asked who she was doing to get an invite to the party. Miss Monroe attempted to get him to keep an eye on the gentleman at the end of the bar, he refused, she reached out to stop him from leaving, and then he asked me to remove her from the party." The guard listed the whole sordid thing as if it was a grocery list, and Lucy wanted the floor to open and swallow her.

Zebadiah never took is eyes off Lucy, watching her color rise as the guard spoke.

"We'll deal with bartender another time, but keep an eye on the man at the end of the bar. I trust Lucy's instincts."

Lucy sagged with relief. "The waitresses," she insisted.

"Eyes will be on his every move for the rest of the evening Lucy, you have my word. Can you make it a little bit longer? The auction is about to start, and I'm expected to bid on something."

Lucy nodded as she took another sip of her wine.

"Good girl, nothing like a little Dutch courage." He took the sting out of his words with a kiss to the top of her head. "Let's go take a peek at what is on offer for the auction, you can tell me if anything is worth buying." He nodded to the security guard and totally ignored Todd, who had looked like he had swallowed a lemon.

Zebadiah led her over to the auction section and they took their time walking around the tables, looking at everything. "What do you think, is there anything worth buying?"

Lucy's eyes landed on a beautiful grey pearl necklace. It was lovely, but she only shook her head. "It's all wonderful. Who donates these things?"

"Businesses, private individuals, sometimes we buy them at deeply discounted rates in hopes that they do well, and we'll recoup our losses. Most of these items have minimums and if they don't make their prices they don't get sold." The band stopped playing and Zebadiah led the way back to their table, waiting for her to sit before he did.

The MC for the evening was full of energy and made everyone laugh including Lucy, although Zebadiah didn't actually laugh, but he did crack a smile.

When the pearl necklace came up on the block Lucy couldn't help it as she leaned forward, eager to see who would win it. The bidding started high and went higher, and her eyes grew wide at the sum of money that was flying around the room. When Zebadiah's voice rang out, joining the bidding, she jumped. The sum that he bid was outrageous, she and her grandmother could live on it for years. She wanted to tell him to stop but she knew it wasn't her place, and as the sum grew she felt her heart start to beat faster.

When the gavel came down on an astronomical sum, Lucy felt like fainting and her heart was racing.

As the applause filled the room, Zebadiah made a motion with his hand, and the MC walked the pearls down to him. He stood and took the pearls, placing them around Lucy's neck, and she jumped at the surprise of it. He fastened them then reached down and adjusted them around her neck, placing his hand against the pearls and her skin, feeling her heartbeat.

She looked up at him as he smiled down at her. "You have a terrible poker face Lucy." He took her chin in his hand and dropped a light kiss on her lips and her world exploded.

Chapter 12

The car ride back to the house was silent. They had left shortly after the auction and as Lucy settled into the car she realized how exhausted she truly was. She rested her head against the headrest and watched the darkened scenery fly by her window. Her hand rested on the pearls at her neck and she loved the way they absorbed the heat from her skin, it was as if they were a living thing. She would be sad to return them when they arrived at the house.

"They suit you," Zebadiah said as he glanced over at her from the corner of his eye.

Lucy turned and looked at his strong hands on the wheel of the car, controlling it effortlessly. "They would suit any woman," she said.

"Did you have a good time?" he asked.

"Yes, thank you," she said politely as her gaze traveled up to gaze at his profile, focusing more attention than she should have on his lips as she remembered his light kiss. It had only been a brief kiss, but it had touched her soul. She moved her hand from the pearls to her lips as she remembered it, and she missed Zebadiah's quick glance in her direction at the movement.

Their conversation exhausted, they rode in silence all the way to the house and the atmosphere between grew tense the closer they got to their destination.

When they arrived, Zebadiah came around to her side of the car and opened the door, extending his arm to her once more. She took it, knowing that it was the last time he would need to touch her.

Lucy ignored the sudden feeling of homecoming as they entered the house, and she headed for the stairs, eager to be out of the overwhelming presence of the man beside her.

"I'll only need a minute," she assured him as she headed towards the room where her stuff had been left. Nothing had been moved and she took her time taking off the beautiful dress and shoes, saving the pearls for last. When she was dressed in her own clothes once again, she took a moment to look at herself in the mirror. Even though she had shed the clothes she still looked different.

Giving herself a mental shake, she picked up her backpack and the pearls which had grown cold then moved across the hall.

Zebadiah was standing with a drink in his hand looking out of the veranda door, and Lucy took a moment to enjoy the gentle breeze that that flowed from one end of the room to other. As if he had sensed her, he turned and let his gaze wander over her changed appearance.

"I left the dress and shoes in the other room," she said, holding out her hand that held the pearls. "I didn't want these to get lost."

"The dress and shoes are yours Lucy, in fact take any of the dresses you want." He didn't reach for the pearls. "Would you like a drink?" he asked.

"No, I have to drive home, and I have no use for the dress, but I do appreciate the offer." She shook her hand with the pearls at him hoping he would get the hint and take the strand.

He studied her for a moment before moving towards the opposite side of the room where his desk sat. When he reached it, he leaned against it, stretching his legs out in front of him, regarding his feet. Lucy noted that he had lost his jacket and bowtie, and his sleeves had been rolled up to show his powerful forearms. He set his drink off to one side and crossed his arms across his chest, turning his gaze back towards Lucy.

"I bought the pearls for you Lucy,"

"No, thank you," she said, holding them out once more. She had the sudden feeling that her wonderful night was about to be ruined.

"I have another proposition for you," he stood suddenly, and Lucy took a step back. "I would like to continue what we started tonight. You attend events with me and...spend time with me when it suits us both."

"Spend time? What does that mean?" Lucy asked, wanting clarification. She wasn't averse to attending other events with him if he wanted.

"I'm attracted to you Lucy and I think we could enjoy one another's company." He took a step towards her and she took a step back.

"You're talking about sex, you want us to have an affair, but only when it suits us?" She felt her entire body go cold. She had a sneaking suspicion that the Monroe curse had once again reared its ugly head.

The Monroe curse was one that affected only the women in the family. They fell in love with impossible men, men that had no interest in a permanent relationship, men that had no trouble taking until there was nothing more to take, and then leaving without a backwards glance.

It was not what she had been expecting after her romantic vision, and the reality of it was like a slap in the face. She heard a door somewhere in the house slam and then another one, and Zebadiah jerked in response to the sudden sound.

Lucy tilted her head looking at him. "It's just the wind," she insisted, knowing it was no such thing. The house was just as insulted by his proposition as Lucy was, perhaps even on her behalf.

"And the pearls," she held up the strand, "they're to be a sort of payment in kind?" Their beauty was suddenly tarnished in her eyes.

Zebadiah's eyes narrowed at something in her tone. "No, they're a gift, no matter what your answer is, I bought them for you."

"No, thank you, to both the pearls and proposition." She walked towards the desk setting the pearls down. "Tell me Zeb, what is so wrong in simply dating someone? Granted, it's a little old fashioned but it's worked for generations."

"Dating generally leads women towards the idea of marriage, and marriage is not an option for me. I like to keep things clear so that no one gets hurt." He moved away from Lucy towards the window as if her nearness upset him.

Lucy didn't dare say that she was already hurt by his offer. He didn't understand that if she agreed to it, everything everybody in town had ever thought or said about her would suddenly be true.

"Things are never as easy as that, and someone always gets hurt in the end," she insisted, turning to leave.

She leaned down to pick up her bag and when she stood, looking back at him, her heart stopped. She recognized this moment. The blood rushed to her ears and she dropped her bag rushing towards Zebadiah. Lucy caught him on the side of his body causing him to spin, he hadn't expected the hit and he grabbed Lucy in surprise as they both lost their balance. As soon as she had rammed her body forcibly into his she heard the glass shatter and then felt a stinging pain in her arm as they landed on the floor with Zebadiah's massive body on top of Lucy.

After a moment, when he could breathe again, he lifted his head and looked down at Lucy, who had closed her eyes at the searing pain in her arm. Once he had assured himself that she was still in one piece, his gaze drifted to the broken window behind them, trying to determine what had just happened. As he realized that they still might be in a dangerous situation his hands went towards Lucy to move her, and as he grabbed her by the arms he felt a sticky wetness and looked down to see that they were both covered in blood.

Chapter 13

Lucy must have passed out because when she awoke she was lying on the bed and she had no recollection of being moved from the floor. She moved to sit up and immediately felt a burning pain in her arm. Looking down, she noticed that there was a piece of cloth tied around it and it was saturated in blood. She raised her hand to remove the cloth and was startled when Zebadiah's hand came down to cover hers.

"Don't, it only stopped bleeding a minute ago, but don't worry, I have help on the way," he explained.

Lucy looked at him and noted he had changed into a pair of jeans and a t-shirt. When she looked around she noted his discarded clothes in the corner and they were covered in blood.

"Are you hurt?" she asked, choking on the words.

"No, but you are, and you need stitches."

Lucy nodded. "Probably, I'll go home and have my grandmother take care of it," she insisted.

"No, you'll stay here and rest, and when you're ready I'll run you home."

"Who is coming?" she asked, having finally registered what he had said earlier.

"Holden Brown, he should be here any minute." Zebadiah walked away from her and Lucy took a moment to look down at her own clothes, they were covered in blood as well, but she didn't care.

She watched Zebadiah as he paced the room, shooting her questioning glances every once and awhile.

"What?" Lucy finally asked, laying back on the big bed.

"How did you know?"

Lucy shrugged, not really wanting to answer that she had seen it in a vision. It would raise to many questions that she didn't feel like answering.

"Was it a set-up, did you get cold feet at the last minute?" He didn't look particularly angry at the idea, only curious, which led her to believe that he didn't believe that a set-up was the answer.

"What do you think?" she asked in return.

"I have no clue, I really don't, are you a witch?"

Lucy gave a sad smile. "No, if I was, my life would probably be a hell of a lot easier."

Zebadiah's phone made a noise and he walked over to where it rested on the desk. "Wait here," he instructed as he left the room.

A few minutes later he returned with Belfort's only doctor. Holden Brown. He was a fairly young man in his early thirty's, about Zebadiah's age, and the two men appeared to know each other.

Holden paused as he entered the room, frowning as he looked at Lucy lying in Zebadiah's bed. He noted her bloody arm and slowly moved towards her, it was as if he was afraid that she was going to bite.

"What happened?" he asked. The question was obviously meant for Zebadiah, so Lucy kept her mouth shut as he slowly started to unwind the make shift bandage on her arm. She had to bite her lip to keep from crying out when he was a bit too rough.

Lucy had never used him as a doctor, nor had her grandmother. She had tried to visit his office once and after getting past the rude staff she found him to be just as rude as they were. That was when she had started to use a doctor in a town that was two parishes away.

"Someone threw a rock through the window and a piece of glass from the window caught Lucy's arm." Zebadiah explained.

Holden twisted her arm so that he could get a better look and she cried out in pain and wrenched herself away from him.

"No more!" she said standing. "You're hurting me, not helping me!" The movement took too much out of her and she passed out once more, landing in a heap on the floor.

******

Zebadiah pushed a stunned Holden out of the way as he scooped her up and placed her back on the bed. "What the hell is wrong with you?" he demanded. His voice was cold steel as he looked over at his friend.

Holden looked from Zebadiah to Lucy with a stunned expression. "You're not having an affair with her, are you?"

"It's none of your business whether I am or not, you're here to treat her wound." He shot Holden a hard look and the man turned back towards where Lucy lay.

"This is more than just glass," Holden said as he examined the wound once more. "It looks like a bullet grazed her?"

Zebadiah didn't say a word.

"I have to report all gunshot wounds," he insisted, looking down at the pale girl.

"It was glass not a bullet," Zebadiah stated frimly. "Just stitch her up please."

Holden frowned once more as he started to take out what was needed to stitch Lucy's arm.

"Out of all of the women in this town you had to choose this one, you never do anything the easy way, do you?" He shook his head.

"Why does everyone hate Lucy?" Zebadiah asked with a false carlessness.

Holden turned to look at him once more. "You haven't heard?" He sounded surprised.

"That she's a witch?" Zebadiah asked with an amused smile. "This isn't the Crucible, women aren't burned at the stake for being supposed witches."

"Maybe she's not a witch, but she is a bit..." Holden hesitated.

"A bit?" Zebadiah cold look zeroed in on Holden, knowing he wasn't going to like his answer.

"Loose."

"Loose?" Zebadiah's voice held a warning in it.

Holden shrugged. "Don't shoot the messenger." He turned back towards Lucy and started to clean her wound which was still bleeding. "She has ruined Thomas Kane, no one in this town understands the hold she has on him. He's married with a child on the way, but he always comes back to her in the end. No one will give him a job in this town because of it. Then there is the man that runs the antique store at the end of the main street, he throws the odd job her way and one can only guess why he does, and the grocer, he lets her shop after hours, keeping the store open late for her." Holden was working quickly. He was good at his job and he wouldn't allow himself to be sloppy even if he didn't care overly much for the patient.

"You've surprised me Holden. I thought you, over everyone in this town, would be more accepting of someone who didn't quite fit into normal society." Zebadiah stared him down and he knew they were both thinking of his partner Mark Peters. They had been together for over ten years, but it wasn't common knowledge because Holden thought it might affect his practice in the little town if he came out as gay.

Holden had the grace to blush at the reprimand.

"My choices don't hurt anyone," he finished up what he was doing then gave Lucy an antibiotic shot.

"Neither do Lucy's," Zebadiah insisted.

"Tell that to Thomas," Holden insisted in return.

Holden reached down and turned her arm to look at his handiwork once more, and Lucy's eyes opened and looked right into his.

"He's the one, you'll be happy." she said with a smile before her eyes drifted shut once more.

Zebadiah knew there was no way she would know about Mark or that they had both been thinking of him.

"What the hell was that," Holden questioned, looking at her from a pale face.

"I'm sure she was only dreaming." Zebadiah responded, walking towards the door and motioning for Holden to follow him. "I'll show you out."

Holden looked at the sleeping woman once more before he turned to follow his friend out of the room. "She'll need to come to the office and have that arm looked at soon, tell her she needs to see me because of the type of wound it is, unless you want it reported to the police."

"I'll let her know," he assured his friend. "Although, she probably won't come unless there is a problem. Why would she?"

"I'm sorry that I've been rude to her in the past, I'll try to be better about it in the future, but you really should stay away from her. She'll ruin you in this town."

"So I've heard." Zebadiah nodded as he opened the front door and scanned the front of the house. "Drive safe and say hello to Mark for me."

Holden nodded and looked as if he wanted to say something else.

"You should know me well enough to know that I will do what ever I damn well please," Zebadiah cut him off before he could drive an even bigger wedge between them.

Holden nodded and got in his car. "Be careful."

Zebadiah nodded and then turned back towards the house. He had to figure out how to get Lucy home to her grandmother, even though it didn't sound as if he could do much more damage to her reputation, a reputation he didn't buy for a minute because she had blushed at his kiss.

As their previous conversation ran through his mind, he recalled her reaction to his proposition of an affair, he couldn't help but close his eyes in frustration. He had royally screwed up with her. An entire town treated her as if she was a whore, and as harsh as a word as it was that was what Holden had in essence called her, and Zebadiah realized he had done the same by buying her the pearls and asking her to have an affair.

He gave half-hearted smile as he recalled her determination in turning him down. No, whatever the town thought, Lucy Monroe was not a whore.

As he entered the study he found Lucy sitting up and looking down at her arm. "Has he left?" she asked, turning her attention to Zebadiah.

"Yes, and I have to get you home. When you're ready, I'll drive you."

"No thanks, I'll drive myself."

"You lost too much blood Lucy, I'm happy to take you. If you don't want me to then I can call Thomas to come and get you if you like," he offered, even though it was the last thing he wanted to do.

"No!" she shook her head. "He's already had enough trouble."

"You can't drive, and you don't want me to take you, is there someone else we can call?"

Lucy shook her head, looking away from him.

"The only other option is for you to stay here until the morning." Zebadiah suggested. "I'll be a perfect gentleman." He held up his hand in a promise.

After a moment Lucy nodded and Zebadiah walked over to a cabinet that held some of his clothes.

"Here is a clean shirt." He tossed it to her. "Do you need help getting to the bathroom?"

Lucy shook her head then stood slowly, shuffling down the hall to the small bathroom. When she returned Zebadiah had changed the sheets and helped her into bed. He tried not to think about how cute and small she looked in his shirt.

"Where are you going to sleep?" she asked.

"Don't worry about me, I have some work to do still. Will the light bother you?"

Lucy shook her head and turned away from him, and he couldn't help but wonder what she was thinking.

He worked until near dawn, then he joined Lucy in the bed, quickly falling asleep despite his worry that he wouldn't be able to with her warm body lying next to his.

When he awoke that next morning, his bed was empty, and she was gone, and he wondered once again just how badly he had screwed things up with her. It was the first time since he had been a very young man that he worried what a woman thought about his actions, but he didn't look too hard for the why because he was certain he wouldn't like the answer.

Chapter 14

It had officially been the worst week of Lucy's life, and she had had plenty of bad weeks in her life to know what one was. It had started when she was shot in the arm. Lucy knew that Zebadiah had lied when he had told Dr. Brown about a rock breaking the window, and she had the stitches to prove it. Thankfully, the wound was healing nicely and there was no infection, so she had no need to visit the doctor once again.

Sunday was only marginally better because she slept for most of the day, too tired and sore to do much of anything else. On Monday, Thomas had cornered her with a New Orleans's newspaper which featured well known business man Zebadiah Abbott and his latest mystery woman. Lucy had to admit that she looked nice in the photo even as Thomas had given her a hard time about dating the boss, and potentially ruining the LeClair job for them both. It had taken all her powers of persuasion to convince Thomas that she had only been doing Zebadiah a favor, and that she didn't think he was the kind of man to put personal feelings over business ones, not that there was any personal feeling involved.

On Tuesday, her mother had called and sunk both Lucy and Etta into a funk as she begged for money and told them that she was better and off the drugs, that she only needed a little help. It was something that they had both heard before and neither one believed her for a minute. Lucy waited full of dread, knowing that since her phone call didn't get her mother what she wanted she would soon come for a visit, and the last time she had done that she had robbed them blind.

When she had gotten home on Wednesday with a bloody hand and sore arm from working to hard, Shy hadn't come to greet her, nor had he returned to the house by Thursday evening, and she was really getting worried. He was a moody dog and had occasionally disappeared, but he had never been gone for two days before. Her worst fear was that a gator had gotten him.

Lucy was never so glad to see Friday, she worked her day, still not having seen any sign of Zebadiah. He had been gone all week and she had been glad of it. The only highlight of her week had been waking up next to him on Sunday morning. He must have crawled into bed very late because he was deeply asleep when she woke. It had taken everything she had to leave his arms. Somehow, during the time that they had slept next to each other, she had gravitated towards him , and when she had awakened her head was on his chest and her leg was thrown over his. She had been glad to get out of the house without waking him, knowing that if he did wake he would insist on driving her home, something she wanted to avoid at all costs.

She had an unreasonable and senseless fear that if he discovered where she lived she would never be safe from him again.

Lucy was in the middle of packing up her things when her phone rang, and she reached into her pocket and answered it while balancing her bag on her knee to close it. "Hey Thomas!" she greeted. Her voice sounded chipper because she was glad the week was finally over.

"Hey Lucy, I got caught up with Hope at her Doctor's appointment-"

"Is everything alright?" Lucy asked concerned.

"Yes, the Doctor is just running behind, but I won't be able to pick up the cake for Etta," he explained.

Lucy felt her heart sink. That would mean she would have to. Etta loved Hummingbird cake and the diner on the main street made the best one in the parish. Lucy had had trouble being served there in the past, so she avoid the place which meant that Thomas bought the cake for her every year.

"It's been ordered and it's in my name and I already paid for it, so you should be able to slip right in and pick it up without a problem." Even he didn't sound too sure at the idea.

"It'll be fine Thomas," she assured him, not wanting him to worry about it.

"You sure?" he asked once more.

"Yep, now go get back to Hope." She ended the phone call before he could worry about the situation any more than he already had.

With a sigh she started for her car, wondering what the odds were that she would be able to get in and out the diner without a problem. As she stepped out onto the veranda behind the house a crack of lightening lit up the sky and a clap of thunder shortly followed it, letting Lucy know that a storm was on the way. Her goal was to beat it home. Maybe if she focused on that she wouldn't be quite so terrified about having to go to the diner.

It had always struck her as ironic that she had been raised with the understanding that everyone in the town was afraid of the Monroes, and the truth was that she was just as afraid of everyone in the town, expect for Thomas and his father, and now Zebadiah, she wasn't afraid of him a little voice reminded her.

As she drove herself into town she let herself wonder what it would be like to have someone like Zebadiah in her life, someone who would handle all her problems for her. She knew was capable of handling them herself, but it would be nice to have someone else take over, just for a little while.

The sky opened up as soon as she pulled into the diner's parking and she had to make a dash for the door, cringing as she heard the bell above it ring when she opened it. She let her gaze scan the somewhat crowded room, noting Zebadiah in the back with Dr. Brown.

Great, now she would have an audience to what she was sure was about to be fiasco.

The woman behind the counter had worked at the diner since Lucy was a child. Her brown hair was tinged with strands of grey and she had it pulled back into a messy ponytail. Her makeup had long ago worn off and she looked as tired as Lucy felt, maybe she was so tired she wouldn't care and would just give her the cake.

She gathered up her nerves and forced a smile to her face as she approached the counter. "Hi, I'm here to pickup a cake under the name of Kane." She was pleased her voice sounded firm if a bit soft.

"You're not Thomas, Lucy Monroe, I can't give you his cake," the woman insisted.

"He asked that I pick it up for him, he got caught in town with Hope." She knew better than to say that it was for her grandmother. "Would you like me to call him so that he can speak to you?" Lucy asked, keeping her tone low and friendly.

"I only have one cake, sorry," the woman said, turning away from Lucy.

"I see it right there in the case, it has Thomas's name on it." Lucy pointed to the spot where it sat in the cold case under the counter.

"Again, you're not Thomas," she shrugged.

"Fine, then I'll buy the cake that is right next to it," Lucy suggested, looking at the second Hummingbird cake that sat in the case."

Her phone rang, and she looked down to see Thomas's number, so she quickly answered it. After a brief explanation to Thomas she passed the phone over to the woman behind the counter, and whatever he was saying was not going over well as the woman turned bright red and her lips grew tight in a firm line.

She handed Lucy's phone back to her then reached into the case to grab the cake and Lucy sighed in relief. The woman was in the process of handing over the box when she released it before Lucy had even touched it and it fell to the floor, making a mess as the box exploded around her feet.

"Oh dear, the woman said with mocking concern, you should really be more careful." Then she shot Lucy a smile so evil that she wondered why she was the one that was called a witch.

"That was your fault," Lucy said in soft voice, not wanting to cause a scene.

The woman only shrugged as if to say prove it.

"Fine, I'll take the cake in the case then," Lucy suggested once more.

"Sorry, that's for the guests that dine in only, and we don't sell whole cakes unless they are ordered."

Lucy walked over the diner's counter and sat down. "I'll take eight pieces of cake please and a cup of coffee." She placed the order with a passive face, but her blood was boiling. "And I expect you to credit back Mr. Kane's credit card for the cake since you were the one that dropped it."

"Sorry, no refunds," the woman said, ignoring Lucy. Lucy sat there for a few minutes before she placed her order again. She started to notice that all of diners in the restaurant had turned their eyes towards her.

She was about to cave and leave the restaurant when she felt someone sit on the stool next to her, and she knew immediately that it was Zebadiah. He turned so that one knee was behind her and the other was in front of her and she suddenly felt safe as his large presence surrounded her.

"Is there a problem here?" he asked softly.

"It's my grandmother's birthday and Thomas always orders the cake," she hated the way her voice sounded so small, "but he had an appointment with Hope and her doctor and couldn't get away." She was doing her best not to burst into tears due to both frustration and embarrassment.

Zebadiah reached up and rubbed her back in an attempt to comfort her. "How's your arm?" he looked down at it, only the edge of the white bandage was visible below her shirt sleeve.

"Fine," she said, taking a deep trembling sigh.

"May I please have two pieces of Hummingbird cake and a cup of coffee to go?" He ordered in a voice that dared the woman behind the counter to object.

Lucy was even more mortified that he had gotten what he wanted so easily.

****

Once the order was delivered she wanted to get out of the diner as quickly as possible and Zebadiah didn't try to stop her, but as soon as she was gone he gave one of his bone chilling looks to the woman behind the counter and asked to speak to the manager, even going so far as to insist that she call him into the restaurant from his home. Then he suggested she clean up the mess she had made in front of the counter before a customer slipped and fell as he rejoined Holden at their table.

"That proves my point," Holden said, stirring his coffee, watching his friend.

"No, all that proves is that this town is full of small minded people who have not been made to face the injustice of their actions."

Holden looked amused. "What is it about this woman that makes you so concerned for her?"

Zebadiah refused to admit that it was the woman herself, it was only the way that she had been treated. He thought of his beautiful mother and how she had been treated in the past.

No, it wasn't fair, and he wasn't going to stand for it.

"Let me guess, you're going to fix it all?" Holden asked, still amused.

Zebadiah gave a cold smile that made his friend shiver a little.

"How are you going to fix it," he asked, resigned to the fact that he was. He had seen Zebadiah get his way too many times in the past to doubt that he would this time.

"I'll buy the whole town if I have to."

"Let's hope it doesn't come to that," Holden said, not doubting that he would do it, and he would do it all for a silver haired woman whether he realized it or not.

Chapter 15

<hr>

As Lucy entered the house she could smell her grandmother's jambalaya cooking and it made her mouth water. Etta had tried to teach her the recipe years before but Lucy hadn't been interested. However, now she thought it was about time that she learned how.

"How was your day?" Etta asked over her shoulder as she removed some cornbread from the oven.

"It was good, I don't suppose you've seen Shy?" she asked as she lifted the lid to the pot that was next to her grandmother and took an appreciative whiff.

"No, but don't worry, he's around," Etta assured her as she looked at the bag on the counter. "What's in the bag?"

"That's your Hummingbird cake. There was a mix up, so I wasn't able to get you a whole cake this year, but at least we have a few pieces."

Etta eyed Lucy, and Lucy returned her look without flinching.

"A piece is all we really need," Etta assured her before she turned back towards the stove. "Go wash up, dinner is just about ready, and I'm hungry."

Lucy looked at her grandmother's back, wondering how much she really knew about what had happened at the diner. They had never discussed what her particular gift was.

It was a warm evening, so Lucy changed into a cotton sundress that flowed around her ankles and slid on some flipflops before rejoining her grandmother to help set the table.

They had just begun to eat when they heard Shy barking furiously at something.

"I told you he was fine," Etta said around a bite of cornbread.

Lucy rose to go check on Shy, wanting to make sure he was in once piece. As she stepped out of the house and onto the dock she immediately noticed Zebadiah standing at the other end with Shy holding him at bay with his menacing barks.

Lucy took her time to study him, even with a growling dog he didn't seem to be deterred in his mission as he took a step towards Shy and Shy took a step back. He looked up and saw Lucy watching him and their eyes met. She didn't know how long they looked at each other before her grandmother joined her.

"He's something, isn't he," Etta said with a smile in her voice, "he's big enough to fight all of your battles."

Lucy jerked at her grandmother's voice, and she realized why she hadn't want Zebadiah to come to the house. She didn't want to get her grandmother's hopes up about a relationship between the two of them.

"Invite him in Lucy, there is plenty of food," Etta suggested before she turned and walked back into the house, leaving Lucy and Zebadiah to stare at each other once more.

"You'd better come in then," Lucy finally said, calling for Shy to come, which thankfully he did.

"I don't think that I have ever had such a warm welcome before," Zebadiah said once he reached her side.

Lucy didn't say anything only turned sharply and led the way into the house. "We were just starting to have our dinner, you're welcome to join us if you like," Lucy offered as she moved to the kitchen to get another place setting.

"Thank you, it smells delicious," he said, being just as formally polite as Lucy was.

It was evident that her grandmother found the exchange amusing as she sat at the table with a smile on her face.

"Zebadiah Abbott, this is my grandmother Etta Monroe." Lucy introduced as she joined them at the table with the extra place setting.

Zebadiah sat a box in front of Etta. "Yes, the birthday girl," he greeted softly. "I believe you enjoy Hummingbird cake," he said as Etta opened the box with a smile.

"I do, bless you." She placed the cake on the sideboard behind her and waved him into a seat before dishing him up a bowl of jambalaya and cornbread. "It's spicy," she informed him before he took his first bite.

He seemed to enjoy it as much as Lucy and her grandmother did, and he ate while he and her grandmother kept the conversation light. They talked a little about the LeClair Mansion and Etta shared some stories of the house from when she was a girl.

Then there as some talk about Shy and what a good guard dog he was before moving on to the house in which she had her grandmother lived.

Lucy had heard it all before, so she was able to let her mind wander about the best way to get him to leave when dinner was finished. She couldn't help but be aware of how his massive body made the house feel full.

"Now Lucy," her grandmother interrupted her thoughts, "it's time for my present."

Lucy really hadn't wanted to give it to her in front of Zebadiah, but her grandmother was determined that she have it now. Lucy stood and motioned for Etta to follow her to the third bedroom in the house. The bed was massive and filled the tiny room, there was barely room to move around it, but it was beautiful. Lucy had painstakingly stripped the wood then stained it once more. The previous stain had darkened over the years giving the bed an almost black appearance, but the new stain had lightened it and made it a warm rich brown once more. Lucy had filled the bed with all down bedding and it looked like a fluffy cloud of white.

"It's beautiful Lucy! It's a bed like I've always wanted!" she crowed as she walked towards it. "Young man help me get into it please," she held out her hand for Zebadiah who held it while she stepped up onto the small wooden steps Lucy had provided.

"Of course, this isn't a bed for an old lady, this is a bed for lovers, Etta said as she settled into the downy softness.

Lucy didn't doubt for a minute that she had said it on purpose, as if planting a seed in Zebadiah's and Lucy's heads. Little did she know that the seed was already planted and had sprouted weeks ago.

"I'm going to lay here for a little while," Etta dismissed them, closing her eyes.

Lucy led the way back into the main room and started to clear the table and lay out the cake plates and forks. "Thank you for getting the cake," she said as she stuck a candle in it.

"You're welcome. I also had Thomas's card credited back for the inconvenience." He started to walk around the room, looking at all the lovely antiques.

"How did you find out where I live?" Lucy asked, knowing the answer before he said it.

"Thomas, but I still don't understand why you fought so hard to keep me away," he said, turning to look at her.

Lucy shrugged. "I didn't want Etta to get the wrong idea."

"And what would that idea be?"

Lucy could feel his eyes drilling into her back. "That there's a relationship between us." Lucy turned around and looked at him, watching him debate about how he wanted to respond.

"I'm sorry Lucy," he said with complete sincerity.

"For what?" Lucy frowned in confusion.

"For what I suggested on Saturday, after the gala. I shouldn't have made the proposition."

"Then why did you?" Lucy was almost afraid to hear the answer, afraid that he would think like the others in town did.

"Because I want you Lucy, its as simple as that. I'm not good at relationships, and I don't care to have a serious one. I thought that if I made the terms clear that you would understand that, but..."

He was hesitant to say anymore but Lucy had to hear the rest.

"But?" She cleared her throat as she waited for him to finish.

"You blushed at my kiss and you refused to take the pearls." This time he shrugged, and she was certain that she was the first person in a long time to see Zebadiah so unsure of himself. "To me, it's evident that you're very innocent, and I don't want to take advantage of that or hurt you."

Lucy blushed once more and looked away from him, confirming his words.

"But I still want you Lucy," his voice was rough as he said it and Lucy felt a tiny thrill course through her at his words. No one had ever said such a thing to her before.

Lucy let her eyes meet his and, although she couldn't say the words, she hoped he could read that it was the same for her.

"The bed is delightful," Etta said as she rejoined them after what felt like only a moment but must have been much longer. "But now I want my birthday cake." She made her way towards the table, seemingly unaware of the tense atmosphere between Lucy and Zebadiah, and waited for Lucy to light the candle.

She and Zebadiah sang happy birthday to her and Lucy enjoyed his deep baritone as it filled the house.

They all took their time eating the cake and listened to Etta talk about past birthdays, but eventually Zebadiah stood and said his goodnights, and the house felt empty after he had gone.

Etta leaned over and patted Lucy's hand before she stood and said her goodnights as well, leaving Lucy to clean up and think about the very big bed in the next room and Zebadiah.

It was as if her grandmother had feed the seed she tried to plant and now it was growing out of control, and Lucy would have to find away to pull it out by its roots before they dug in to deep.

Chapter 16

It had been a few weeks since she had seen Zebadiah and she wasn't sure if he was keeping his distance on purpose or if he was busy with business matters. Somehow, she felt it was the latter because he didn't strike Lucy as the type that would shy away from an uncomfortable situation.

Thomas's baby girl came two weeks early in the middle of July. Lucy was pleased to hear the news, and Thomas had sent her a photo. She knew she wouldn't be welcomed to see the baby in person, and she tried her hardest not to be disappointed by it.

He had been gone for only a week and in that short time the LeClair project had turned into a nightmare. Thomas's assistant foreman, Steve, had taken over management of the site while Thomas spent some time at home with the new baby, and Steve had no interest in listening to the suggestions that Lucy had made to Thomas at the beginning of the project. He had decided that he was going to make his own mark and impress the big boss by speeding up the progress of the work and making sure that they were ahead of schedule. He didn't particularly care that corners were being cut either.

Lucy was between a rock and a hard place. She could call Thomas and tell him what was going on and in the process, alienate Hope more because she would see it as Lucy being jealous and unable to let Thomas spend time with her and the new baby. On the other hand, when Thomas returned and realized the many accidents that were occurring and the corners that had been cut he would be mad that she hadn't called to tell him

Lucy heard a loud crash and glass breaking on the floor above her and cringed at the words that she heard ringing around the house. The workmen had been in the study installing some of the HVAC duct work, and she had a feeling that they had broken the glass on the front of one of the enclosed bookcases. The glass was original to the house and irreplaceable.

Her instinct was to run up there and stop them and had she been anyone but herself she would have. She had already tried to intercede a few times to keep unnecessary mistakes from happening, but she had been told to shut her mouth and stay out of their way or she would find herself without a job. Lucy wasn't sure if Steve could fire her, but she figured if she at least kept an eye on things she could tell Thomas all that had been done incorrectly, and she knew for a fact some of the mistakes were costly.

There was another crash and more foul language as Lucy cringed.

"What the hell was that!" Zebadiah asked from the foyer. Lucy had finished with the drawing room and had moved across the hall to the dining room. The beautiful wainscoting had all been painted white many times and the thick paint was proving difficult to remove.

"My guess is it's the glass doors to the cabinets in your study," Lucy said in a clam voice as she looked over her shoulder. It was pouring rain outside and he hadn't taken the time with a rain coat or umbrella, and she couldn't help but enjoy that way his white dress shirt was plastered against his large shoulders and arms.

"And you're just sitting there, letting them break all of that historic glass?"

"I tired to stop them earlier, I was basically told to shut up or get out. I figured if I stayed I would at least know what they screwed up so that it could be fixed." She shrugged.

"And the site, it's a mess out there, there is litter and sawdust everywhere, and who moved the port-a-lets so that they're the first thing you see?"

The sound of air compressor and pneumatic nail gun suddenly started up and Lucy cringed at the noise.

"Where is Thomas?" Zebadiah demanded as he started for the stairs.

"He's on vacation, his wife had the baby, he's only been gone a week," Lucy defended him, and Zebadiah turned around on the bottom step to look at her as she yelled over the noise. "He put Steve in charge."

"And you didn't think to call him about this fiasco?" Zebadiah shouted.

"And have Hope track me down and kill me? No thank you," she shouted back.

When they heard a buzz saw start they both cringed, but then as suddenly as it all started it stopped as the power in the house switched off, leaving them all in the late afternoon's overcast dimness.

"There, the house took care of it," Lucy said, turning back towards her work as she heard the muffled curses from above once more. She listened as the shouting grew louder when an argument started about having too much running at once and blowing a breaker.

Lucy knew that wasn't it, it was the house, and she didn't doubt that the house wasn't going to allow the power to be turned back on until the situation was corrected.

It had been weeks since she had seen Zebadiah, and she had been nervous to see him once more because of what had happened the last time they had been together. It wasn't everyday that a man admitted that he wanted her, and she wasn't sure how she should act towards him now.

However, when she had seen him she hadn't felt the least bit awkward, and it hadn't felt as if he had been gone for over two weeks, it felt as if she had seen him only hours before.

Zebadiah let his eyes wander over Lucy in her baggy overalls before he turned towards the feet pounding down the stairs. Lucy looked over her shoulder just in time to see Steve meet Zebadiah at the bottom. It was too dark in the room to be sure, but she was thought that he had turned a vivid red.

"How is everything going?" Zebadiah asked with icy cold politeness, and Lucy had to cough into her arm to disguise a laugh. She had been, thankfully, forgotten and she watched over her shoulder as Steve looked from Zebadiah back up the staircase.

"F-f-fine," he stuttered as two other men came stomping down the stairs.

"It doesn't sound or look like it's going fine?" Zebadiah said with a tilt of his head.

She swore she saw Steve's knees shaking and she wondered how Zebadiah could make grown men shake in their boots and not frighten her in the least. In fact, she found the entire situation amusing.

Steve looked over Zebadiah's shoulder to the front door as if judging his chances to make a clean getaway.

"Leave the site, everyone!" Zebadiah insisted in a hard voice, and the three men needed no further encouragement. "And don't return until you hear from Thomas that it is alright to do so," he said as they disappeared around the corner.

Lucy waited silently as she heard Steve shout something over the rain at the few other men working on the site. When she heard their cars start up one by one and leave the site she stood, placing her five in one tool on the floor beside her.

"Would you mind if I have a look at the damage, or would you prefer me to leave as well?" she asked calmly.

He stood back from the stairs and motioned for her to proceed him. There was a window with a window seat at the top of the first landing and she took a moment to look at the torrential rain falling outside the window.

"Is Etta alright with all of the rain? She's not going to float away, is she?" he asked, moving to stand behind her and look out the window. She could feel the heat from his body and she swore she felt his hand brush hers.

"She's fine," Lucy assured him, knowing that Etta had survived much worse than a thunderstorm in her house.

She continued up the stairs and her shoulders fell when she saw the mess in the study. She rubbed her forehead as she looked at the two busted cabinets, even the mullions that held the glass had been broken. There were large holes in the plaster ceiling that were obviously much larger than the vents that would be placed there, and she couldn't help but wonder how they had planned to patch them, and absolutely everything was covered in plaster dust.

In all, there were six broken panes of glass and the mullions would have to be custom made.

"I'm sorry Zeb," she said, kneeling to pick up the worst of the glass.

"Don't Lucy, you'll cut yourself. Besides I want Thomas to see this mess in all it's glory." Zebadiah said as he pulled out his phone.

Lucy wandered over to the window doing her best to ignore the pane of glass that was covered with plastic. She listened to Zebadiah call Thomas, insisting that he come at once before ending the call.

"There, now he can deal with it and you won't have to be the bearer of bad news, so Hope can't blame you," Zebadiah said, leaning against one of the unbroken cabinets, watching her.

"No, but Thomas will," Lucy said sadly, and Zebadiah didn't disagree.

"Why didn't you want Dr. Brown to report my bullet wound, that is what it was, right?"

"Yes." He looked at her as if debating how much he wanted to say.

"You don't still think I was a part of it, do you?" she asked in a wavering voice.

"No, I don't," he assured her. "I didn't want Holden to report it because I wanted my private security to look into it before I told the police. Especially because I think it might be a police that did it," he explained.

"You think it was Joel Brantley?" she asked with a shiver.

"Possibly, but there are a few other choices, I have a lot of enemies." He shrugged.

"And a lot of ex-lovers," Lucy supplied.

He grinned. "Yes, there are a few of those, and you did cause quite a stir at the gala," he agreed.

"That's what I like best about you Zeb, you're so humble." She laughed.

"I was paying you a compliment," he said with pretend hurt.

There was a heavy pause between them and his eyes narrowed. "Why do you call me Zeb instead of Zebadiah?" he asked suddenly, completely throwing Lucy off balance.

"I don't know, it's just how I hear your name in my head," she explained. "Why? Would you like me to stop?"

"No, only a few people call me Zeb," he explained without really explaining anything.

There was a tense silence between them once more and Lucy realized that he didn't let just anyone call him Zeb, and she couldn't help but wonder what that meant.

She cleared her throat after a minute. "I have some extra panes of glass that we can use to repair your bookcases," she offered.

He didn't say anything, he only continued to stare at her until she couldn't take his intent look any longer. "What!" she insisted.

"I'm just wondering if you realize how lovely you are?" he asked.

Lucy blushed at his words. "Don't say things like that," she begged, moving towards the door to get away from him, but he reached out and grabbed her arm.

"Did you miss me this week Lucy? Because I missed you." His voice dropped to a warm rumble and Lucy felt it in her tummy.

"Why are you doing this?" she hissed, desperate to get away from the affect he was having on her. "I thought we agreed that this wasn't going to happen, that there would be nothing between us?"

"I don't recall agreeing to such a thing, I do recall apologizing for my earlier offer of an affair, but that is all that I recall." He rubbed his thumb against the inside of her wrist and he had to be able to feel the pounding of her heart.

"It meant the same thing." She pulled her arm out of his grasp as she heard Thomas shout up the stairs.

Zebadiah must have seen the look on her face because he gave a wicked smile. "Saved by the bell,"

Thomas entered the room and couldn't help but pick up on the tension in the air. He looked between the two of them before the room around them caught his attention.

"What the hell happened here!" he shouted.

"That's what I want to know," Zebadiah said, taking one last long look at Lucy before he turned his attention to Thomas.

"I'll be downstairs if anyone needs me," Lucy excused herself, making her getaway, much as Steve had done earlier.

"Don't go too far Lucy," Zebadiah said without looking at her.

It made Lucy want to run as far and as fast as she could.

Chapter 17

Zebadiah watched as Lucy left the room, giving her a moment to get down the stairs, while Thomas turned his attention to Zebadiah. After a moment, when he realized that Zebadiah wasn't going to start the conversation, he took a long look around the room noting all of the damage with a grimace.

"I'm sorry about this, I obviously chose the wrong man to take over the job while I was away. I'll be in first thing in the morning to get this all cleaned up and get the job back on track," Thomas assured him.

Zebadiah noticed his uneasiness, and he didn't want to be the cause of more stress than he probably already had with a newborn at home.

"Look Thomas, I would rather this job take a few months longer to complete than I had anticipated then have it done incorrectly or have corners cut. Which is obviously a message that Steve didn't receive." Zebadiah took a long look around the room and the chaos that surrounded them.

"How long were you planning on taking until you returned?" Zebadiah stood up from where he had been leaning on the desk and walked towards the window, taking the time to assess the damage In the ceiling above it.

He didn't see Thomas wince as he noticed a slice in the wall plaster that looked like the jigsaw had slipped.

"I was going to return the week after next, but I don't think that I would feel comfortable taking the time now." Thomas looked away as Zebadiah glanced over at him.

"Let's tag team it then," Zebadiah suggested. "I will be around next week, you come for an hour in the morning and an hour at the end of the day and I'll be here the rest of the time. Perhaps my presence will deter bad decisions by your crew."

Thomas looked at Zebadiah, his shock at the offer easy to read.

"I'm happy to keep an eye on things if it will help," Zebadiah assured him. "Congratulations on you daughter by the way."

"Thanks on both counts, and that schedule would work," Thomas agreed quickly, not wanting to look a gift horse in the mouth.

"However, Steve must go, I wouldn't trust him to complete any job he started, and it would be a waste of our time to have him here. I know I would always be following behind him to make sure he was doing his job." Zebadiah looked at the hole in the ceiling once more. "Wasn't the HVAC crew supposed to do this?"

"No, I was going to have a guy I know that specializes in plaster come and cut the holes next week when he does the other plaster work. I wanted him to be able to repair as he went because the plaster is old and likely to crumble."

"Just as it did here." Zebadiah nodded his approval at his plan.

"I can only guess that Steve's idea was that he would get your HVAC installed sooner and that would make you think he was capable," Thomas said. "What I don't understand is why Lucy didn't call me and tell me what was going on before all of the happened, or at least try to stop them."

"She did try to stop them, and Steve suggested that she keep her opinions to herself," Zebadiah regarded Thomas as he wondered how far he wanted to take the conversation. "Can you really not guess why she didn't call you to let you know?"

Thomas gave a self-mocking smile. "I can guess," he said. An answer which neither confirmed nor denied a relationship with Lucy, and he decided not to push for an answer.

"Do you want me to take care of Steve for you?" Zebadiah asked.

"No, it's my mess, I'll clean it up. I'll have the crew here to clean up this mess tomorrow, but it will probably take them the rest of the week to sort it all out.

"And get the power turned back on," Zebadiah added.

Thomas looked around realizing it was out for the first time. "I'll see to that before I leave," he assured him.

"If the house will let you, according to Lucy it's not a given that she will," Zebadiah stated with a completely serious face, and he could tell that Thomas was trying to figure out how he had taken Lucy's comment.

"Thanks for your help with Etta's birthday cake. I never did thank you." Thomas continued to watch Zebadiah closely.

"You're welcome, I enjoyed meeting her, she is a delightfully outspoken woman." This time Zebadiah did give a small smile at the thought of the little woman who looked so much like Lucy. "And she makes a very good jambalaya."

"She makes the best. You had dinner with them then?" he asked casually.

Zebadiah looked up at Thomas from where he had been studying the cut in the wall. "Yes," was all he said, and he could tell that Thomas was dying to ask him more, so Zebadiah patiently waited for him to do that very thing. Perhaps the questions Thomas asked would let know what was between him and Lucy. He didn't have to wait long.

"I saw that she attended the Abbott Gala with you."

"She did," Zebadiah confirmed, still not giving anything away.

"Are you bothered that people call her a witch?" Thomas asked, it was not a question that he had expected, and his surprise must have shown. "I'm sorry if I offended you, but I'm curious."

"I asked her if she was a witch and she denied it." It was a remark that he was sure Lucy would have found amusing, but Thomas took the statement seriously as he nodded in response.

"You believed her?" he asked, wanting a definitive answer.

"Yes, it made total sense when she explained that if she was a witch her life would be, 'a hell of a lot easier', was I believe how she put it." Zebadiah moved around the desk to stand across from Thomas.

"She said that, that doesn't sound like her," Thomas said thoughtfully.

Zebadiah didn't think it was a good time to mention that she had just been grazed by a bullet when she said it.

"She does have a gift though," Thomas supplied, and Zebadiah felt as if it was a test.

"I'm beginning to notice that," Zebadiah leaned against the desk once more in a casual manner, inviting his confidence.

"I don't understand it fully, and neither does she, but she can see the future but only sometimes."

Zebadiah nodded having gotten one of the answers he wanted, but he was starting to feel uncomfortable talking about Lucy behind her back. "That explains a few things," he said, ending the conversation by starting a new one.

"Why don't you go see about the electric and I'll hunt down a broom and a dustpan?" Zebadiah suggested.

"What, about Lucy?" Thomas asked, wanting to continue the conversation and wanting to know what it explained.

"What about her, I'm sure she's left for the day," Zebadiah said, deliberately misunderstanding the question as he started towards the door.

Thomas was forced to follow him down the stairs where they found Lucy packing up her stuff for the day.

"Did you two get it all sorted?" she asked, looking up from her task.

"We did," Zebadiah assured her, "and we both agreed that you can keep your job. Now, if you wouldn't mind having a little one on one discussion with the house while Thomas tries to get the power turned back on, I would appreciate it."

Lucy's eyes narrowed as she looked at him.

"Where is a broom and dustpan?" he asked, changing the subject.

"I last saw one on the veranda." Lucy supplied, looking between the two men.

Zebadiah couldn't help but think that she looked kind of cute when she was riled, and he could tell his comment had riled her.

"Lucy, why don't you come with me to the breaker box in the kitchen?" Thomas suggested, seeing the same angry sparks in her that Zebadiah did.

"Fine, but then I'm going home. I'm not staying to help clean up the mess upstairs," she insisted, stomping off towards the kitchen as Zebadiah walked in the opposite direction.

He couldn't help but think that he had missed her while he had been away, and that he was glad he would be around the following week.

Chapter 18

<hr>

"What the hell is going on between you and Abbott?" Thomas hissed as he led the way towards the kitchen which was at the rear of the house.

"Nothing is going on, I haven't even laid eyes on the man for over two weeks!" she hissed back.

Thomas muttered something under his breath as he stepped over the mess that included extension cords, saw horses, lumber, and even a few bricks. "Why didn't you bother to tell me what was going on here?" he grumbled, pushing a sawhorse out of the way so that he could get to the electrical panel.

"And have Hope kill me, no thank you," Lucy returned. "How is the baby by the way?"

"She's beautiful, perfect, wonderful!" Lucy could hear the smile in his voice even though his back was to her.

"Show me a photo," Lucy insisted and waited as Thomas pulled out his phone and pulled up the photos before he handed it over.

Lucy scrolled through the photos with a smile as Thomas flipped switches with no luck.

"I don't suppose anyone thought to turn the tools that were on upstairs off and unplug them?" she asked offhandedly while she flipped through the photos.

Thomas muttered an oath, and Lucy couldn't help but grin at his mistake.

"You're tired," Lucy reassured him. "But even if you do unplug everything she probably isn't going to allow the power on until the site is set to rights."

"Is there a problem?" Zebadiah asked from across the room, looking a the two of them.

"I don't suppose you remembered to turn off everything upstairs?" Lucy asked him over her shoulder.

"I just did, what does the power situation look like?" Zebadiah said, not missing a beat.

"Nothing, I don't know what the problem is?" Thomas said, scratching his head.

"I told you what the problem is, clean everything up tomorrow and try again." Lucy handed Thomas back his phone and turned to leave.

"Where are you going?" Thomas wanted to know.

"I'm off the clock, I'm going home," Lucy said

"I thought you didn't work by the hour only by the job?" Zebadiah quirked an eyebrow and Lucy bit back a grin at the move, wondering if the fierce look he was now giving her worked in the boardroom.

"Ok, then, electrical work isn't in my contracted job description," she parried as she pushed by him.

"You've discussed your job description with Mr. Abbott?" Thomas asked, shocked at the idea.

"Yes, I caught her working late one night and I was concerned about overtime, and her being here alone, but she reassured me it wasn't a problem," Zebadiah clarified.

"Lucy, you were here by yourself!" Thomas all but shouted.

Lucy shot Zebadiah a quelling look. "You promised you wouldn't tell!" she hissed.

"I don't believe I promised, agreed maybe, and only because it was convenient at the time," he explained.

Lucy's face turned bright red in anger and she stomped past Zebadiah, her movement's jerky as she gathered up her stuff because she was in a rage, and both Thomas and Zebadiah followed her into the room, watching her.

"Thomas, would you please excuse us?" Zebadiah requested.

Thomas looked from one to the other and nodded, moving onto the front porch and closing the door behind him. At his departure the air in the room grew tense as Zebadiah and Lucy stared at each other.

"I'm sorry Lucy, I shouldn't have said anything. I'm a sore looser and you had one upped me with your comeback," he said with all sincerity.

"And that was the best that you could come up with!" she exclaimed in disbelief.

He gave a very crooked and charming smile that made Lucy melt a little bit. "I don't like arguing you with."

"But you're O.K. with Thomas arguing with me?" She really didn't get the man.

Zebadiah took a step towards her and Lucy took a step back in self-defense.

"I only want to see your arm," he said, reaching for her hand and drawing her close.

Lucy held her breath as his hand trailed up her arm lifting her sleeve. The bandage was gone and so were the stitches, but the skin was still red and angry. He let his thumb trace the scar and she sucked in her breath at the sensation of his caress.

"Does it still hurt?" he asked, his eyes searching hers.

"No," she assured him, shaking her head and licking her lips, watching as his dark eyes turned black with desire when he realized why she had gasped.

His gaze fell to her lips and he pulled her a little closer to him, forcing Lucy to tilt her head back to look up into his eyes. She didn't want to stop looking into his eyes.

His hand came up, tracing her cheek, then his thumb traced her lips while his other arm gathered her close, and all the time his eyes never left hers.

She could feel his breathing deepen to match her own as she waited for him to make his next move.

When the power suddenly came on they both blinked, and Lucy jumped back in surprise, looking around, expecting to see Thomas watching them.

"I guess the house decided to forgive," Lucy said softly, having to clear her throat.

"Or she's trying to save me from making a mistake," Zebadiah said, turning to look behind him as Thomas entered the house. He didn't see Lucy's quick look of hurt at his words.

Leaning down, Lucy picked up her bag and left while Zebadiah and Thomas were talking about the sudden return of the power. She had gotten to the end of the veranda when Zebadiah and Thomas stepped out on to it.

"Lucy?" Thomas called.

"I'm going home before anymore mistakes are made!" she said, forcing a cheerful note into her voice, ignoring the frown that crossed Zebadiah's face at her words. Perhaps he thought that she had said too much.

Well, that was just too bad, she would continue to say what she meant because she always had.

She held back the tears as she climbed into the car and started the engine, but before she could pull away Thomas was knocking on her window, forcing her to roll it down.

"Come by the house tomorrow night. I want you to see the baby."

Lucy shook her head. "I'll come when Hope issues the invitation and not before." Then with a soft good night she started to roll up her window, forcing Thomas to step away from the car with a frown.

She should let that be a reminder, if Thomas's wife Hope didn't want anything to do with her, why one earth would Zebadiah? She held back the tears until she reached the end of the drive. She was so sure he was going to kiss her. Stupid!

****

"What was that all about?" Zebadiah asked as Thomas rejoined him on the veranda.

"I want her to come and see the baby, but she won't until Hope invites her." Thomas walked past Zebadiah and through the hall, towards the front where his car was parked.

"Why won't Hope invite her?"

"Hope is a few years younger than us, and she believes everything that she has ever heard about Lucy. She hates that Lucy is my friend, and she's jealous."

"Does she have a reason to be?" Zebadiah asked, no longer able to hold the question back. He had a feeling that his thoughtless words had hurt Lucy. He didn't think the kiss would have been a mistake, but the timing would have been.

"You mean the rumored affair that Lucy and I have been having?" Thomas shook his head with a sad smile. "Little minds in a little town," Thomas said opening his truck door. "I love Lucy and I always will, but if I had wanted to marry her I would have, a long time ago."

Zebadiah watched Thomas as he climbed into his truck and drove away. He had only answered the question of a current affair, he hadn't answered the question about a past one.

Zebadiah rubbed his face, taking in the fresh air that had been cleansed by the rain. Scanning the area and seeing nothing amiss, he entered the house and started to lock everything up as he went. He would have to at least get his bed cleared if he was going to stay.

It would be easier to drive back to the city and stay there, but he wanted to see Lucy first thing in the morning to explain. His phone buzzed in his pocket and he pulled it out to look at the message. It was Summer and it was a 911; he had an early meeting scheduled. It was a crucial deal and the other side was trying to pull power plays and a last-minute meeting was their way of trying to catch him off guard and unprepared.

But he was always prepared, at least in business matters. Silver eyed witches were a completely different animal however.

Chapter 19

Zeb had needed someone to attend and important business dinner with him, and Lucy had agreed before she had thought about the consequences. All she could think about was that she wanted to spend more time with Zeb, and that he had offered her the chance to do that, and that is why she now stood in front of a full-length mirror at Zeb's New Orleans row house admiring another lovely dress picked out by Summer.

This one was variegated colors ranging from a pale blue to a deep purple, and it floated around her like a cloud. It was tea length and once again sleeves with a wrap made of the same material. The shoes were ballet flats, so she wouldn't have to worry about keeping her balance all night.

"I think you missed your calling Summer." Lucy turned to look at the woman behind her who was clearing up the mess she had made.

"You're fun to pick out clothes for because of your unique coloring, I've never seen anything like it," she said letting her eyes wander over her hair and eyes. She had cut her hair for her and applied her mark-up artfully once again.

Lucy sensed that there was something wrong with Summer, she didn't seem as carefree as she had the last time they had met. "Is something wrong

Summer?" she asked turning to look at the woman as she sat heavily on the bed behind her.

Zeb had given them the spare room to use. The row house was beautiful but small. Zeb had told her that it was only a temporary home, he had bought the entire row of houses to restore and then sell, and he could sell a lived-in house easier than a vacant one.

Summer remained silent behind her and Lucy moved to join her on the bed. "Do you want to talk about it?" When she saw Summer look at her searchingly she smiled reassuringly. "I promise, I'll not repeat a word."

Summer closed her eyes and sighed. "It's really not all that big of a deal but it feels like it is one." She stood up and started to pace.

"Sometimes not being able to share something can make it a bigger deal than it really is," Lucy said softly.

"I've been dating a man for about six months, and it's been going good. Now he has a job offer in another city and he wants me to come with him, but I'm not sure that I should." Summer sat next to her on the bed once more. "He's always been jealous of Zebadiah, he thinks that there was or is something going on between us." She shrugged. "I have told him that there is not nor has there ever been anything remotely romantic between me and Zebadiah, but he doesn't believe me." Summer had told her the same thing when they had last time but she was glad that she had stated it more clearly.

"New relationships often make people a little insecure, there has to be time to be sure of the love that someone claims to feel for you." Lucy said, giving the man the benefit of the doubt.

"Sure, and I thought about that, but I love my life here, and it would be giving up an awful lot for someone who can't believe me when I tell them the truth." Summer shook her head as she said the words.

"That sounds like you've made up you mind," Lucy said with a smile.

Summer took a deep cleansing breath. "It does, doesn't it?"

She grinned in relief and Lucy reached over to pat her hand, her stomach bottoming out as she touched her. She could see red all around Summer, her beautiful hair in a pool of it, Lucy broke into a cold sweat and her eyes dilated while she looked through Summer as the vision refused to leave her.

"Lucy!" Summer shook her shoulder to get her attention, but Lucy didn't feel it, and when Summer tried to pull her hand away Lucy tightened her grip as if to keep her next to her and safe. "Lucy!" she shouted once more as she tried to free herself. "Zebadiah!" she called when her second attempt didn't work.

Zeb was there in an instant, kneeling in front of Lucy, touching her arm softly as he said her name, and that was all it took for her to snap out of it.

Everything came back into focus as Summer tried to pull her hand away one more time and this time Lucy let go, snatching her own hand back.

"Sorry," she said, "I must have had a little panic attack." It was how she had explained away her visions in the past. "I must be more nervous about tonight then I realized." She gave a weak smile at Summer's look of concern.

"Thank you, Summer," Zeb said as he looked up at her. "We'll just sit here until Lucy feels better."

Summer looked a little relieved to be let off the hook, and she walked over to where she had left her oversize purse. "You're sure, I can stay longer if you need me to?" she offered as she shot Lucy a concerned look.

"No, I'm fine," Lucy insisted once again. "It happens from time to time, and I generally bounce back quickly."

Summer walked towards the door, but Lucy stopped her before she reached it. "Thank you, Summer, once again you worked miracles, and I love the dress."

Summer gave her a smile then left, and Zeb waited until he heard the front door close before he sat next to Lucy on the bed.

"What happened Lucy?" Zeb asked taking her hand, knowing it wasn't a panic attack. She had had the same look in her face when she had told Holden he would be happy, but there had been no smile on her face this time only panic. "What did you see?" he asked.

Lucy looked at him shocked. "See?"

"Yes, you had a vision. What did you see?"

Zeb was looking at her with complete seriousness, he wasn't teasing her.

"How did you know about my visions?" Lucy asked, jumping up.

"Thomas told me you can see the future but only sometimes. What did you see, it didn't look good did it?" He waited as she paced, absorbing the news that Thomas had shared her secret.

The fact was that she needed to tell someone what she saw, and she couldn't tell Summer, it would at best alienate her, and at worst scare her to death. But Zeb could take care of it, he could keep an eye on her and keep her safe.

Knowing that she was about to reveal something about herself that she never shared with anyone, she took a deep breath and looked at Zeb, who was patiently waiting for her to continue.

"I can see the future, but only if I'm present at the time that a decision is made that will affect the future. Sometimes it's through touch and other times it's eye contact." She sat on the bed next to Zeb, thinking about how best to tell him what she saw.

"The man at the bar at the gala, you saw something?" Zeb questioned.

"Yes, he was carrying a body and stuffing it in a trunk." She shuddered.

Zeb nodded. "We caught him putting something in one of the waitress's drinks behind the bar."

Lucy nodded, knowing that he would have taken care to make sure that the man was reported to the police.

"What about Summer, what decision did she make?"

Lucy shook her head. "I promised not to tell you, and it doesn't matter what the decision was, but I..."

"It's alright Lucy, I'll believe you," he reassured her.

Lucy felt like crying in relief, but after so many years of keeping her wall up to protect herself she could let it down enough to show him how thankful she was that he would.

She took another deep breath. "I saw red."

"And red is bad?"

"Yes," she said softly. Thinking of the vision she had had when she has first met him, the image of him being shot.

"What did you see with the red?" Zeb asked, taking her hand once more, rubbing his thumb across the back of it in a soothing manner.

"I saw all of her beautiful hair in a pool of red." This time Lucy did cry, and she wiped away the tears, as if she was ashamed to let him see them.

Zeb grew tense beside her. "Is there anything else you can tell me?

"We were talking about her current boyfriend. Do you know him?" Lucy looked up at Zeb who was frowning.

"Yes." It was clipped, and Lucy got the impression that Zeb didn't like him.

"You don't like him?" she asked.

"No, not particularly, he's the jealous type and is convinced that Summer and I are having an affair."

Lucy felt herself relax a little, if he knew that much than he could figure out the rest of it.

He turned to Lucy, raising his hand to wipe away a tear. "I'll take care of it. Do you still feel up to going out? I have to go but you don't." He smiled at her tenderly and she couldn't help herself, she wrapped her arms around his neck and hugged him tight, almost afraid to let go.

After all these years, to finally be heard and believed, it was such a relief.

Zeb held her close, his big arms surrounding her, making her feel safe.

"Thank you," she whispered before pulling away suddenly shy.

"You're welcome," he said, rising and moving away from her. "Am I on my own?" he asked once more.

"No," Lucy shook her head, pleased that he was giving her an out if she wanted one, but she didn't want one, she wanted to be with him. "Give me five minutes to fix my make-up then I'll be ready."

Zeb nodded. "I have a few phone calls to make so I'll be in the other room. Join me when you ready."

Lucy nodded sitting down at the dressing table and looking at her tear streaked face. All she needed was a little powder and some more mascara. It only took her a few minutes, but when she was finished she sat looking at herself in the mirror, wondering if what had just happened had really happened or if she had dreamed it all.

To have Zeb believe her made her heart fill with hope. Maybe others would believer her too.

Chapter 20

Lucy felt Zeb's hand in the middle of her back as he guided her from the car and into the restaurant. He had filled her in on what was going on in the car. The woman he was attempting to make a deal with was pretending to be unsure of herself, but she knew exactly what she wanted. Zeb was waiting for her to tell him what it was. However, in the mean time he was dealing with a lot of feminine power plays.

The reason he had asked Lucy to accompany him to dinner was to try to make the meeting less about business and more social, he admitted that it was a power play on his part, one he wasn't sure would work.

Lucy looked around the restaurant, listening to the jazz trio as she did. It was housed in an old warehouse that had been completely gutted and rehabbed. The rough brick and stained concrete floor were muted by candle light, plush seating, and crisp white table cloths.

There was a healthy mix of couples and business parties scattered around the restaurant all talking in muted tones. She couldn't help but note the flurry of activity as Zeb entered the restaurant. The hostess glided up to him and whispered something in his ear before he nodded to the maître d' who led them to a table by one of the oversize windows in the back.

"Marissa," he greeted, holding out his hand.

A very short and round woman rose from the table they were led to and took his hand. Her hair was a wild wavy mass that had a multitude of highlights in it. She wore a stylish pair of glasses and her outfit was well tailored.

"Zebadiah, I was wondering if I had made a mistake about the date," she said in an overly sweet voice that immediately rubbed Lucy the wrong way.

Zeb gave a charming smile, but Lucy could see the hand by his side clenching and unclenching as he kept careful control of himself over the passive aggressive comment.

"Zebadiah is too much of a gentleman to pass on the blame, but it is completely my fault," Lucy said just as sweetly as Marissa had as Zeb held out her chair. Lucy could play passive aggressive and insincere sweetness just as well as the next person. She was born in the south after all.

"Marissa Langford, please meet Lucy Monroe. I hope you don't mind my bringing her this evening, but I don't get to see enough of her, and I wanted to have this evening be less about business and more about enjoying good food with friends," Zeb smiled as a waiter appeared by his shoulder.

Lucy watched as he said something softly to him and he disappeared.

"I was excited when you mentioned this restaurant for dinner. I've been hearing wonderful things about their chef for months, but it's almost impossible to get a reservation." Marissa looked around her, noting a few of New Orleans's well-known citizens.

"I was lucky," he said, not really answering the questions as some menus were delivered along with glasses of water, and a few minutes later a bottle of wine.

They took their time looking over the menu and savoring the delicious wine before placing their orders. Lucy was sure that it didn't matter what she chose because everything would be delicious, delicious and expensive.

Marissa turned her attention on to Lucy, looking at her over her glass of wine. "What do you do my dear?" she asked.

Lucy heard the witches voice from the Wizard of Oz in her voice, saying 'I'll get you my pretty...'. It was ironic since she was the one that was supposed to be the witch.

"I restore furniture," Lucy responded, keeping it simple because she really didn't want the woman to know anything about her.

Zeb must have picked up on her unease because he directed the conversation away from her and back towards more mundane things such as current city events and people that they both knew.

Lucy felt a hum of energy and it was so strong that she looked up and into and man's eyes who was waiting alone at a table. He looked nervous and he gave her an anxious smile. Something caught his attention by the door and Lucy watched as a grin split his face.

Images flashed before her eyes and she zoned out of the conversation at their table for a moment as she saw moments of his life flash before her, it was going to be a happy one.

"Are you alright?" Zeb asked, leaning over and whispering into her ear. His warm breath on her neck gave her goosebumps.

"Yes." She nodded as she looked up at him with a happy smile.

There was some fleeting emotion that crossed his face that Lucy didn't recognize as he looked down at her, but he quickly masked it as he turned his attention back towards Marissa.

On her other side Lucy heard a guest apologizing to the waiter and asking him if there was anything that he could do, the more she listened the more she realized that she didn't want to hear. The poor man's credit cards had been declined, he had no cash to pay, and he was with his wife who couldn't help.

The hostess appeared by Zeb's side as if by magic, blocking the scene at the next table from Lucy. What Zeb whispered to the woman was a mystery, but she nodded and disappeared just as quickly as she had appeared.

As dinner was served Marissa gave up on trying to keep it social and they launched into the business deal. Most of it went over Lucy's head, but she got that it was a real estate deal and that Marissa was lying about the viability of it. Nothing as vulgar as numbers were being mentioned, but Lucy had the distinct impression that they both knew what price range the other was aiming for.

Lucy had just set her fork down and was picking up her wine, her eyes meeting Marissa's, and she couldn't miss the look of satisfaction that flickered there, but what she saw next made her drop her wine, spilling it on the table.

She closed her eyes against her third vision of the evening, she couldn't do it anymore, she need a dark and quiet room. She saw a courtroom, newspaper headlines, and reporters everywhere. They were all surrounding Zeb, and this woman was the reason why.

Some of the wine must have landed on Marissa because she jumped out of her seat quickly brushing at her skirt.

"I'm sorry, how clumsy of me," Lucy said weakly.

Marissa muttered something under her breath and then excused herself.

"Let's dance while they clean our table," Zeb suggested taking her hand and pulling her gently from her chair and onto the dance floor.

He moved her around the floor in time with the slow music and Lucy felt herself relaxing and growing tired. She felt safe, and wanted to stay in his arms forever.

"How did you get us reservations?" Lucy asked looking around the room one more time, careful to avoid the people in it.

"I own it," he said as he spun her around.

Lucy gave an unladylike like snort. "Figures."

"You don't seem impressed," he teased.

"You also took care of the couple with the declined credit cards meal, didn't you?" She knew the answer before she even asked the question. He had done it so quietly that no one had noticed, and she doubted that the couple he had helped even knew what had happened.

He shrugged. "Why did you smile earlier?" he asked, changing the suject.

"The man was going to propose to his girl and they were going to be happy," Lucy said with a smile, resting her head against Zeb's shoulder.

"Does that happen often, seeing people's futures?"

This time Lucy shrugged. "I do my best not to look at people. It's only when I look at them or touch them that it happens."

"You looked right at Marissa before you dropped your wine," he noted as he stopped dancing and looked down at her.

"Yes," she agreed, lifting her head off his shoulder to look up at him.

"What did you see?"

"Reporters, courtrooms, bad press and you in the middle of it all." She stepped away from him as a horrible thought crossed her mind. Could he possibly be using her? He had readily believed in her gift which was a new experience for her, but had he brought her here this evening to determine if he should make the deal or not?

His eyes narrowed as he noted her withdrawal. "Are you alright?'

"No, I'm tired and have a headache, can we leave soon?"

Zeb looked over at their table where Marissa now sat, waiting for them.

"Sure, give me a few more minutes and I'll get you out of here," he assured her.

"Will you take me home?" she asked, knowing that wasn't what they had agreed to, they were supposed to stay in the city for the night and go home in the morning.

She watched as Zeb's face lost all expression and his hand dropped to his side. "Sure, if that's what you want," he agreed.

Lucy nodded, it wasn't what she wanted, but it was what she needed. She needed to be away from him to think about everything that had happened.

Chapter 21

Lucy was sitting by the river with her lunch spread out around her as she leaned against a tree listening to the water flowing along the bank. Reaching for an apple, she bit into the crispness, enjoying the sound it made as she broke a piece off with her mouth.

It had been two weeks since she had gone to dinner with Zeb, and while she had seen him passing, they hadn't had much to say to each other. She wasn't exactly sure who was avoiding who though.

As if he had read her thoughts, Zeb sat down beside her. "You've been avoiding me," he said softly, picking a blade of grass and playing with it. She watched his long graceful fingers as they smoothed the blade between them.

"Funny, I was just wondering why you were avoiding me," she said, taking another bite of her apple.

He looked out over the water, he smiled, but it didn't reach his eyes. There was something bothering him and she had a feeling that it had to do with her since he had taken the time to seek her out.

"What's wrong?" she asked, offering him some of her apple, but he waved it away.

"I looked a little deeper into Marissa Langford's past business dealings, and there was a very unsettling trend." He turned to look at her, this time he really looked at her, his gaze searching her face as if he was looking for answers. "How did you know?"

"I told you what I saw," she shrugged. I didn't know exactly what it meant though.

"And then you wanted me to take you home, why?"

Lucy threw her apple into the river, wondering briefly if fish liked apples.

"You believe my visions, you trust me, but I don't trust you," she said honestly, feeling him tense beside her. "I'm sorry if that hurts your feelings, but I can't help it."

"Is it because of the proposition that I made that night, do you think that I have the same mindset of some of the other people in this town?"

"Perhaps, but there is a small part of me that worries that, because you believe in my visions, you might be using me for those visions. You might have taken me to dinner that night to get a read on the situation."

"I honestly hadn't thought about it that way, I thought you were afraid to stay the night in my house alone with me," he said with a frown.

"No, I'd be more afraid of myself in that instance," Lucy whispered as he looked at Zeb out of the corner of her eye. She heard his deep intake of breath, and she watched his eyes spark at her words as the atmosphere grew heavy between them for a few moments while they each thought about what could have happened if she had stayed with him.

Then he laughed and broke the spell. "I'm relieved that it wasn't because you're afraid of me," he said softly.

"But you're O.K. that I don't trust that you're not using me?" Lucy was perplexed by his attitude.

"No, I get that, part of me still thinks that you might me using me a little too, for my money."

"Get that a lot, do you? Poor Zeb, it must be tough to be sooooo rich." She sighed.

He smiled again as a comfortable silence developed between them and they both watched the river for a time.

"Have you heard anything more about who shot at you that night?" Lucy asked as she started to pack up her things.

"No, but I have a few suspects that we're looking into," he assured her.

"Can I ask you something Lucy?" He placed his had on her arm, stopping her from finishing what she was doing, and Lucy eyed him warily.

"I promise Lucy, if I ever want you to use your gift to try to read something or someone I will make sure to ask your permission first, although sometimes I think that it will happen anyway, like it did with Marissa."

Lucy looked at his eyes which were full of complete sincerity, and she nodded her agreement.

"But how do you keep it from happening, when you go to places like parties and restaurants?"

"I keep my head down and don't look at or touch anyone," she explained.

"Isn't that hard?" he asked.

"Yes, that's one of the reasons I stay here in Belfort, I know everyone here, and I know how to avoid them for the most part. It can get overwhelming in a big city, especially the bad stuff."

"How is it that you don't know who shot at me?" Zeb looked tense as he awaited her reply. "How did you not see yourself getting shot?"

Lucy sat down next to him once again. "Maybe I haven't met them, or maybe I wasn't near them when they made the decision."

"But you saw me getting shot in a vision?"

"Yes, but I rarely see myself in a vision and it was a split-second decision that I made the moment I realized what was happening." She shrugged. "I don't understand how the visions work all of the time."

"When did you see me getting shot? I was there when you had the vision?" He turned sideways to look at her and his face was inches from her. She could see the dark stubble under his skin and the little lines at the corners of his eyes.

Her heart stopped and then started quickly, she couldn't tear her eyes away from his.

"The day I met you," she said softly, not thinking about the answer.

"You had other visions that day too, didn't you? One made you blush." He reached up and traced her cheek as she blushed again at the thought of it.

She cleared her throat. "Yes."

"Tell me?" he asked softly as his thumb moved to her lips.

"The first one was when you came up the stairs, I had a vision of you and two little dark headed girls." She left out the part about herself and being pregnant.

"My nieces," he assumed with a smile.

That wasn't how she had read the vision, but Lucy didn't correct him.

"And the other?" he asked gently.

Lucy shook her head. She would not tell him that one.

"Maybe one day you'll tell me, when you trust me more?" He pulled her to him, causing her to lose her balance and she fell into him. His arm came around her, holding her close as his lips descended on hers.

It wasn't a gentle kiss as his hand lifted to her head to hold her close.

Lucy didn't fight him and her arms snaked around his neck. She had waited so long for him to kiss her again, and as he deepened the kiss she gave a little cry of delight matching his intensity with her own.

"Am I interrupting something?" Thomas asked from behind them and Lucy jumped but Zeb held her tight, not letting her go as he looked down into her eyes.

"Yes, you are. May we have a few minutes?" Zeb requested, his voice hard.

Lucy felt guilt washing over her, she had promised Thomas that there was nothing between her and Zeb, and there really wasn't, but he would think that she had been lying to him.

Thomas stomped away, and Lucy tried to jump up to go after him, but Zeb wouldn't let her leave his arms. "What's between the two of you?" he asked.

Lucy pushed hard against him and he let her go quickly. She wouldn't look at him for fear she would see something she didn't want to see.

"A lifetime of trust!" she hissed, scrambling to her feet.

She had to find him and explain. She didn't look back as she raced up the hill. Her lips were still burning from Zeb's kisses, but she didn't dare look back.

She didn't have to because he was right behind her all the way to the house.

Chapter 22

When Lucy rounded the front of the house and caught up with Thomas he was already surrounded by the crew which meant Lucy couldn't talk to him alone.

"The storm has changed track, it's expected to land anywhere from Texas to Alabama which puts us in the center of the cone." Thomas looked over at Lucy and Zeb as he spoke. Lucy guessed that was why he had come looking for her. "We need to start preparing for a direct hit. I don't want to leave it until the last minute because I know you all have your personal property to see to as well. We'll get as much done as we can today, and if we don't finish today we'll finish tomorrow morning. The projection is that they will start voluntary evacuations tomorrow evening with mandatory, if needed, the following day."

Lucy felt her stomach heave a little at the news that the storm had changed course, she had lived through plenty of storms and hurricanes, and she dreaded every one of them.

Thomas was starting to break everyone into teams and handing out assigned areas of work. After everyone had dispersed Lucy walked over to Thomas, seeing her chance to talk to him.

"Thomas," she said softly as he turned towards the sound of her feet on the gravel.

"Are you staying to help?" he asked, looking over her shoulder at Zeb, and Lucy noted something that passed between them, but she wasn't sure what it was. "I wasn't sure if you had anything that needed to be taken care of in New Orleans."

"I'll stay here and help," Zeb said.

"Lucy, do you and Etta want to go with Hope and me when we leave tomorrow?" Thomas asked. It was evident that he wasn't going to talk about the kiss that he had witnessed between her and Zeb.

"No, I doubt that Etta will leave, and I'll have to stay." Lucy shook her head, knowing that if her grandmother had yet to be beaten by a storm there was no way she would leave.

"This is a massive storm Lucy, she can't stay, they are forecasting a CAT three at the very least!" Thomas's voice was full of frustration.

"I know, but she has never left for a storm before, so she won't now, but we both know a lot can change with a hurricane in three days. We'll have to hope for the best." Lucy looked at the beautiful sky above her. The thing about hurricanes was that they pulled all the bad weather into their system which gave one a sense of false security; for how could there be a monster storm just off shore when the weather was so beautiful?

"The stubborn old woman," Thomas muttered under his breath.

"You're preaching to the choir Thomas. I'll try to get her to leave, just like I try every time, but I doubt she will go." Lucy shrugged. "Thomas, about what you saw-"

"Lucy, it's none of my business," Thomas assured, her turning to leave.

"I agree, but I told you a few weeks ago that there was nothing between Zeb and I-"

"The Zeb in that statement would suggest otherwise, but again, none of my business." He started to walk away with Lucy walked next to him, and thankfully Zeb didn't follow.

"I didn't lie, not then," she promised.

"And now?" he asked, stopping to look down at her.

Lucy looked over her shoulder at Zeb, who leaning against Thomas's truck, watching them.

"I don't know, he believes in me, he trusts me when I tell him stuff." She shrugged, turning back towards Thomas. "I like him a lot and I had a vision..."

"A vision?" Thomas's voice was sharp. "What of?"

"Of him and me," her voice was so soft.

"I thought you never had visions that involved yourself?" He frowned.

"I never have before, but..." Lucy looked over her shoulder at the powerful man behind her, "but, Etta also told me something my aunt said when I was born, 'Her life will be blessed, and she will be content when the name which begins with the ending and ends with the beginning arrives.'"

"I don't get it?" Thomas said, "And what was your vision?"

"His initials are Z.A., the end and the beginning of the alphabet. In my vision I saw him in the house with two beautiful little girls and me. We were putting the girls to bed and-" she swallowed.

"And?"

"I was pregnant." As she said the words aloud her heart started to race at the image. The thought of her and Zeb, their lives being that interconnected made her almost giddy. She took a steadying breath. "I want it to be true Thomas, but I'm guarding my heart against it."

"Why?"

"Because what if its not, what if he's using me, what if I saw it wrong?" She felt like crying but she didn't. She didn't say that she was also lonely, or that she wanted to love and be loved. He had Hope, and he had never had trouble dating, or having relationships. He had never led the lonely life of an outcast.

"That's a whole lot of if's Lucy," Thomas said softly.

Lucy also didn't say that Zeb wasn't offering a relationship only an affair.

"I wanted you to know that I didn't lie," she repeated her earlier statement.

"Lucy, I worry about you, and I don't think that he is the type of man who sticks around very long. I hope I'm wrong and that your visions are true, you deserve to be happy. I only ask that you be careful."

Lucy nodded. "I will be Thomas, but I think I'm too far down the path to turn around."

Thomas nodded. "Let me know if you talk some sense into Etta," he said. Having said his peace, he wasn't going to discuss it anymore." Then he turned and walked towards the back of the house.

It only took a second for Zeb to join her. "Is the trust still there?" Zeb asked softly.

"I think so, I hope so,"

"You love him." It was a statement not a question.

"Yes, he's the only real friend I have ever had, the only one, besides my grandmother, who believed in me," she turned to look at him, "until now."

Zeb must have read something in her eyes that he didn't want to because he closed his and sighed. "I'm afraid I've already hurt you Lucy. I didn't want to but you're so...there's something..."

Lucy was amused to see a hesitant Zeb once again, she didn't think that it was something that happened often and now she had witnessed it twice.

"Innocent, yes I know, you've said it before." She nodded, watching something flare in his eyes at her words.

"No, I was thinking intoxicating, alluring, bewitching, there's something about you that overrules my ability to think rationally." He stared at her wide eyes and blushing cheeks. "See, if I were thinking rationally I never would never had said those things." His hand pulsed by his side

Lucy had never wanted anyone to kiss her as much as she wanted him to kiss her in that moment. He stood so close to her, looking down into her eyes as he tried to guess what she was thinking.

She felt she should say something to acknowledged what he had said, but she wasn't sure what that might be, and after a few more moments of silence he stepped away from her and the mood was broken.

"Do you think you could talk Etta into weathering out the storm here at my house instead of yours? At least it wouldn't be on the water and there aren't as many trees around."

Lucy swallowed hard, touched by his offer. "Thank you, I'll ask her."

Zeb nodded, giving her a bit of a lopsided grin before walking away.

Everything in her heart said to run after him, but she wasn't sure what the point would be.

Chapter 23

The storm was headed right for them. A voluntary evacuation had been done the day before and the parish had now called for a mandatory evacuation . They were an hour northwest of New Orleans which offered them a little more safety but not much. Lucy had been pleading with Etta to leave for the past twenty-four hours. She hadn't mentioned Zeb's offer yet, she had been saving it as a last resort, and unfortunately she was finally there.

"Etta, we have to go somewhere safe," she pleaded with her stubborn grandmother one more time.

"I have lived through more storms than I can count, and all of them right here in this house. I have no interest in leaving." She shook her grey head once more. "But if it makes you nervous, you go."

Lucy closed her eyes in frustration. "You're being unfair, you know that I could never leave you here. The worry would be worse than staying through the storm."

"I've made my choice child, I leave you to make yours."

"Would you at least consider going down the road to LeClair and waiting out the storm there? Zeb has a generator and the house isn't under all of these trees, nor is it right over the water."

Her grandmother stopped to look at her, considering the option and Lucy held her breath, waiting.

"If the roads are closed you could walk home after the storm if you needed to, it's only a few miles down the road," Lucy coaxed.

"Will Zeb be there?" Etta tilted her head as she waited for Lucy to answer.

"He didn't say, but I imagine so, it would be safer than staying in New Orleans. Why?"

Etta looked away from her. "I wouldn't feel right staying in the man's home if he wasn't there too."

"So, you'll consider it?" Lucy asked, feeling a sense of relief.

"What about Shy?" Etta asked.

"We can try to take him, but he's already hunkered down, somewhere. He did this last time remember? He disappeared a few days before the storm and came back a few days after, but if we're at Zeb's it'll be easy to get back here and check on him right after the storm." Lucy assured her.

A knock on the door startled her and she turned to see Zeb standing on the other side of the screen. He was wearing a t-shirt and jeans, as if he had come expecting to help board them up if necessary, but Lucy had already taken care of that the day before.

"I take it you're not leaving Etta?" he asked, waiting to be invited into the house which Etta did.

"No, I've lived through too many storms to be afraid of this one."

Lucy rolled her eyes in frustration at her words, she had heard it all many times before. Zeb looked as if he was about to disagree, but Lucy shook her head to tell him is wasn't worth it. He wouldn't say anything she hadn't said in the past.

"Will you at least consider coming to stay with me at my house?"

"You're sure you wouldn't mind having us?" Etta asked, meeting his eyes. "You have plenty of room?"

"Yes, it's a big house. There will be a few others staying as well and I borrowed some cots from Fred Kane at the church. He'll be staying along with Thomas, Hope, and the baby."

Now Lucy didn't want to go, and both Zeb and Etta must have sensed that as they looked at her.

"My sister and her little girl will also be staying too, but there is plenty of room."

Etta nodded. "We'll come along later then," she said, moving toward the kitchen. "We have some things to do here first."

Zeb looked at Lucy. "Where's Shy?" he asked.

"He always takes off before a storm, he has somewhere he goes. I think it would be more stressful for him trapped in a house with strangers than it would be for him to be out on his own in the storm."

"If you want me to help look for him I will," he offered.

"No thank you, he would run from you anyway."

He looked as if he wanted to say something else, but Etta was pulling out stuff in the kitchen behind them. "Walk me out?" he asked.

Lucy nodded and walked with him down the pier and towards the car. When they reached it he turned and leaned against the car crossing his arms.

"Is there anyone local that you can think of that might want me gone or out of the LeClair house?"

"Is this about being shot at?"

Zeb nodded, looking down at her. "In part, but there have also been a few other things that have happened around the house and site."

"Such as?" Lucy asked, turning to lean against his car as well.

"Minor petty things, flat tires, broken windows, all things that could be contributed to a work site but seem to happen to frequently to be accidental."

"What about Joel Bradley?" he asked.

"He definitely has the personality for it, but I can't imagine what he would have against you?" Lucy shook her head. She had thought about it and it didn't make sense.

"I'm keeping him from you, he thinks I'm stepping on his turf," Zeb suggested.

"No, he's a bully and likes to harass me, but he wouldn't be caught dead with me in this town, on any level." She shook her head.

"It doesn't mean he doesn't want you Lucy. The fact that he does and can't have you makes you even more desirable." Something in his voice made Lucy look up at him and she saw fire in his dark eyes.

She wanted to tell him he could have her, he could easily maker her his any time he wanted. All it would take was a simple kiss.

"Is there anyone else?" he asked, getting back to the subject.

"Perhaps the shooter and the vandal aren't the same person, did the vandalism at the house happen before or after Thomas fired Steve? He doesn't fit the timeline for the shooting, but maybe everything else?"

"It's a thought," he said.

"What about your girlfriend Gianna? You said she had stalker like tendencies."

"Maybe." He sounded like he had already thought about that. He stood and moved towards his car door. "Call me if you need help with anything and remember the curfew, sundown."

The parish had issued a curfew after the mandatory evacuation to keep people off the roads and out of trouble.

"Thank you for taking us in Zeb," Lucy said as he climbed into his car.

"Is it worth a kiss?" he asked with a grin.

"Probably, I'll let Etta know she owes you one, I'm sure she'll be happy to oblige!" Lucy laughed as she turned and walked away with a smile on her face. It was a happy moment in a day fully of worry which would only get worse as the storm approached.

Chapter 24

Lucy and Etta were staying in the kitchen. It wasn't fully completed, but it had the basics which allowed them to cook up all the food they had brought with them. They had beat the curfew by an hour, and not long after they had arrived Zeb's sister, Zelda, had arrived with her daughter Eden and Gianna, whom had claimed to need a safe place to stay during the storm.

Gianna must have imagined a romantic scene between her and Zeb as they survived the storm together because she was shocked when she walked into the full house. Zeb had given her a friendly enough greeting, although there was no smile, and informed her she would have to share a room with Zelda and Eden. Neither Eden or Gianna looked pleased at the idea.

Hope had been civil so far, they had shared a friendly greeting between them, but Lucy hadn't felt brave enough to ask her if she could hold the baby, and Thomas had been too busy with last minute preparations to insist that she should.

Thomas was in the same situation that Lucy was with her grandmother. His father refused to leave, insisting that the church would need to open immediately after the storm to provide a safe place for those who would need one. Thomas had begged Hope to take the baby and leave, but she had no interest in leaving him or traveling alone with a new born.

The storm was still about six hours out, but the wind had picked up and the rain had started as the outer edges of the storm bands had started to reach them. Eden thought the entire thing was an adventure and had settled into the kitchen to help Lucy and Etta. Etta was cooking a gumbo to use up the seafood and sausage she had frozen. It would provide a hot meal, maybe the last for a few days once the power failed.

Lucy was making biscuits and scones for breakfast the following day, using up the rest of her butter and milk in the process, and Eden was enjoying cutting out the shapes for the pastries.

"There you are," Zelda said as she joined them along with Gianna. She walked over to her daughter and placed a kiss on the top of her head while she watched her work.

Lucy wondered what had happened to Eden's father, but she couldn't figure out a polite way to ask the question

"Where is the child's father?" Etta asked, not worried about being polite.

"Etta!" Lucy hissed in warning.

"It's fine Lucy. He died shortly after Eden was born, Ms. Etta." The oven beeped, and Zelda walked over to remove the biscuits that were done, picking up another tray and sliding them in to bake.

"Eden, I think those biscuits need a taste test." Lucy suggested as she reached into the refrigerator and pulled out some of Etta's homemade apple butter.

Eden grinned as she waited while her mother helped her prepare the biscuit.

There was a sudden gust of wind and the lights flickered causing the atmosphere in the room to change as everyone suddenly remembered the storm that was bearing down on them.

"Gianna, would you like a biscuit?" Zelda asked, taking a bite of Eden's.

"No, thank you," she pursed her lips. "I think I'll just go make sure Zebadiah doesn't need any help."

"Who peed in that girl's cheerios?" Etta asked as she added some extra spice to her gumbo.

Zelda coughed on her bite of biscuit, her eyes meeting Lucy's with amusement.

"I think she's upset that there are so many people here," Zelda said in order to play peacemaker.

"She fancies your brother?" Etta asked.

"Probably, most women do," she agreed.

The lights flickered again, and Eden grabbed her mother's hand as she realized that it might not be all fun and games.

"You know what we need?" Lucy asked, moving to her bag in the corner and pulling out her tablet. "We need some music to bake to, it will make the food taste better." She found one of her favorite play lists and started the music. It immediately lightened the mood and they continued to bake and sing along to the songs as the weather outside the house grew worse.

****

Zeb stopped outside the kitchen, watching the women as they worked The situation outside was growing worse but they had created a little oasis in the kitchen. The music was turned up to drown out the wind and rain and the smells were delightful.

He didn't doubt that it was Lucy's doing as he watched her grab Eden's hand and twirl her around to an old seventies tune. Eden was giggling, and her face was smeared with jam.

He may not have Lucy's ability to see the future, but he did know what felt right, and it felt right to have her in his home with his family. It felt right to have her in his life.

His heart started to beat as if he had just run a marathon, he watched her throw back her head and laugh and he knew. He was in love.

His sister looked up and caught him looking at Lucy, and she moved to join him before he realized he had been spotted standing in the shadows. Lucy and Eden were so busy laughing that they didn't notice anyone else.

"There's something about her, something in her spirit, it reminds me of mom," Zelda said as she wrapped her arm around Zeb's waist.

Zeb nodded. "She's had similar hardships to Mom," he agreed.

"Ah yes," Zelda looked over her shoulder to make sure no one was listening, "the witch thing. Gianna filled me in on that one."

"It has made her an outcast in the community..."

"Just like Mom was in her own," Zelda finished for him.

"I noticed some tension between her, Thomas, and Hope," Zelda said, smiling as her daughter started another fit of giggles.

"Thomas and Lucy grew up together and they're still close, and it has created rumors in the town about the two of them. Hope either resents it or is jealous, but I can't tell which it is."

"Are you jealous?" Zelda nudged her brother.

"A little," he agreed.

"Well she has my and Eden's approval." Then she sighed heavily. "I'm sorry about Gianna, but what was I going to do? Leave her?"

"Don't worry Zelda, it's fine," Zeb threw his arm around her shoulders which caught Lucy's attention.

Their eyes met and held for a few seconds before she smiled at him.

"Zeb," Lucy called, "come and try one of Eden's biscuits, they're delicious."

"She calls you Zeb," Zelda said, shocked. Their mother was the only one who had ever called him Zeb, the only one he would allow to call him Zeb

"Maybe there is a little witch in her," he whispered as he grinned down at his sister before he moved into the kitchen. "They smell delicious, as does the gumbo Etta." He included her in the compliments.

"Lucy said you wanted a kiss as payment for us staying here," the older woman said, eyeing him as he sniffed over her shoulder.

"I might have mentioned it." He smiled at the woman, feeling relaxed and happy despite the storm raging outside the window.

Etta lifted her cheek, and Zeb picked up the cue and gave her a kiss on the cheek. "But I think that's me kissing you?" Zeb corrected her.

"Yes, and that's me allowing it." Etta said with all seriousness.

"Now me!" Eden said running over to her uncle and lifting her arms. Zeb lifted her gave her a big loud smack as well. "Now Mommy!" Eden cried, tugging her mother into the circle and Zeb dropped a kiss on his sister's head as he hugged her.

Bless the little girl she was playing it so well.

"Now Lucy!" Eden said. They all knew it was coming and Zeb heard Etta chuckle, pleased that her plan had worked. "You can't leave her out!" the little girl insisted.

"No, I can't, can I?" he said as he grabbed her arm and pulled her close.

'It's fine Zeb, I don't need a kiss," she insisted, blushing as his arms wrapped around her.

She felt wonderful. He looked down at her. "Nope, you owe me payment just like everyone else." He said as he quickly captured her lips before she could think of something smart to say.

And he was lost in her taste.

A few moments later when Eden giggled it broke the spell, and as he pulled away he noticed that she looked as shell shocked as he felt.

"Dinner is ready," Etta said, turning away from the stove. "Eden, go round up everyone and tell them dinner is ready."

The little girl was eager to help and left the kitchen in a hurry.

Zeb stepped away from Lucy as Etta handed him a bowl of food, but his eyes never left Lucy.

Chapter 25

Lucy was cleaning the last of the mess in the kitchen when Thomas entered, holding the baby.

"Would you like to hold her?" he asked as moved towards her.

"Where's Hope?" Lucy asked, wiping her hands on her pants as she reached for the baby.

"I told her that I was going to come spend some time with you and let you hold the baby. She decided she was going to take a nap while she had the chance." He gently handed over the baby and Lucy cuddled her close.

"She's beautiful Thomas," she said with tears of happiness for her friend.

"I'm worried about you Lucy," Thomas said after a few minutes of silence. As if the world had heard the ominous tone in his voice, the wind rattled the shutters that were closed against the storm.

"Why? I'm fine Thomas," Lucy insisted as her body began to naturally rock the baby.

"It's you and Zebadiah he's so cold, I worry that if you fall into a relationship with him that you will get hurt. I can't see him loving anyone, at least not for very long." Thomas watched her carefully. "I know that you had a vision, but are you sure it wasn't just wishful thinking?"

Lucy thought about the early scene in the kitchen, he had been anything but cold then.

"What did you and Zeb talk about that night up in his office?" Lucy asked, "I noticed that he took over the job for you the following week, is that the act of a cold man?"

"It's the act of a man that wants his house finished and is willing to help, I never said he wasn't a fair man, only a cold man." Thomas shook his head. "We talked about a few different things."

"Me?" Lucy asked.

"In part, I asked him if he believed you were a witch."

"What did he say?" She held her breath.

"He said that he believed you when you said something along the lines of, if you were, your life would be a hell of a lot easier. I told him that didn't sound like you."

Lucy smiled. "Would you worry less if I assured you that he is fair, and that with me he is anything but cold."

"He's warm and cuddly then?" Thomas snorted in disbelief.

"No, he's gentle and kind, and considerate of my feelings and wellbeing. He takes care of me and keeps me safe. He also believes me when I tell him about my visions."

"So, you told him about your vision?" Thomas asked, shocked.

"Only part of it, I left my part in it out,"

"Why? If he's so great and believes in you, why wouldn't you tell him?"

Lucy shrugged. "It's complicated."

"You're afraid he won't believe you, admit it."

Lucy turned her back to Thomas only to find Zeb leaning against the doorway watching them. She froze wondering how much of their conversation he had heard. By the look on his face it must have been most of it.

"The questions I have are how much and what exactly did you leave out of the vision Lucy?" he said, his voice quiet, and she jumped at the sound of it.

Thomas spun around and looked at Zeb, but Zeb hardly noticed because his eyes were glued to Lucy.

"Why don't you come up to my study when you and Thomas are finished here?" Zeb suggested and then turned and left as silently as he had arrived.

Lucy handed back the baby and then closed her eyes in mortification.

"You'll have to tell him the rest of that vision now," Thomas said unhelpfully as he stood with the baby.

"Go take care of your wife, Thomas," Lucy said, turning to finish the last of the cleaning. After he left she drew it out for as long as see could, but when the kitchen was as clean as she could make it, she realized that she had to go because if she didn't he would track her down.

She slowly made her way up the stairs in the quiet house, almost everyone was in bed, trying to get some sleep before the worst of the storm started, most of them hoping they would sleep through the worst of it.

Zeb's door was open and when she peeked her head in he looked up from his desk. "Come on in and close the door," he requested.

Lucy did so, slowly and when she turned toward him he had moved around to her side of the desk, leaning against it, his head tilted questioningly.

"Did you need something?" Lucy asked, clearing her throat.

"Would you come over here please?" he asked, watching her. "It's your choice Lucy, but I would appreciate it if you would." He gave her a gentle smile and she melted. As soon as she reached him he pulled her between his legs, wrapping his arms around her waist.

"I heard what you said to Thomas," he started and when Lucy opened her mouth to interrupt him he placed a finger on her lips then turned it into a caress as his thumb followed his finger.

"You're not wrong Lucy, but neither is Thomas. I am kind and gentle with you, I want to be considerate of your feelings and wellbeing, and I most definitely want to take care of you, and if I'm honest I've never felt the need to be any of these things with anyone outside of my family. There is something about you that makes me want to protect you at all costs. However, I'm also a cold man with most people, I've had to be to get where I am today."

Lucy opened her mouth to speak and he silenced her once again. "You don't have to tell me anything you don't want to, I trust you to tell me when your ready to or when you think I'm ready to hear it, whichever the case might be."

"Stop Zeb!" She ripped herself away from him. "It's too much too fast!" She wanted to be in his arms, she wanted him to kiss her, but how did she know it wasn't all an act? Maybe he was cold, cold and charming, and he knew exactly the right thing to say to get what he wanted from her.

"Don't you trust me Lucy?" He didn't seem mad only confused by her withdrawal from him.

She sunk onto the chair behind her and Zeb waited patiently. The only sound in the silence was the wind and rain as it picked up, mimicking the churning feeling in her gut.

"You're right when you say I'm innocent Zeb, there were no boys in this town that wanted me, and in the big city, well it was too hard to really connect with anyone, I always had to be on my guard. I found out, before things ever really began, what men wanted, I could see it. I never saw myself, but I always saw them walking away so I never wanted to get...close."

Lucy heard him take a deep breath.

"How do I know you're different? I don't," she answered her own question, "you could just be much better at hiding it than they were. You've already admitted that you don't want a relationship only a friend, but now you've changed your mind and it feels almost like you're courting me, to use an old-fashioned expression, and it confuses me."

"Your vision, were you confused when you saw it?" he asked.

Lucy shook her head. "No, it was very clear." She looked at her hands as the memory ran through her mind. "All of them," she said softly.

"Don't trust me Lucy, trust yourself, trust your vision." He knelt in front of her, taking her hands. "I want you Lucy, and I am trying very hard to give you the rest of it, the courting, your vision, whatever it might be, I want to give you all that you want, but it scares me just like it scares you."

"I find it hard to believe that you're afraid of anything Zebadiah Abbott." She smiled weakly.

"I'm very afraid of hurting you," he said simply.

Their eyes met, and Lucy realized that if she was ever going to take a chance in her life this was the time to do it. She reached her hand up and traced his face, his cheeks, eyes and lips. He closed his eyes at her touch and she could see the pulse in this throat leap, its erratic beat matching her own.

She lowered her lips to his gently and it was like setting fire to a candle, they both went up instantly. Zeb stood pulling Lucy with him, taking control of the kiss. She wanted more but she wasn't sure how to ask for it. She had never been in a situation like this before.

"Zeb," she pleaded when he pulled away.

"No, not here not now," he insisted, his voice rough, and as if to prove his point there was a knock at the door.

He took a deep shaky breath before heading towards the door of the study.

"Zebediah, I don't suppose you would keep me company? I'm ashamed to admit that I'm afraid of the storm." Gianna gave a self-deprecating laugh. She looked over his shoulder and caught sight of Lucy who stood staring at her with unseeing eyes, shocked by what had just happened between her and Zeb.

She couldn't help but wonder what it all meant. Did it mean he had feelings for her, that he cared?"

Gianna's face turned red and she cleared her throat. "Sorry, I didn't realize that you were with someone."

"Yes, Lucy and I were trying to work on a few things," Zeb said vaguely.

"Well then, I'll leave you," Gianna said, turning abruptly and leaving.

Zeb shut the door and turned to look at Lucy. "Stay here with me tonight?" he asked. "I have a feeling that it's going to be a long one, and I think if we spent it together it might go a little bit faster.

Lucy smiled and shook her head. "You're afraid that if I leave she'll come back."

"Yes, and I would much rather have you here than her."

"I would much rather it was I who was here," Lucy said honestly.

He turned off the main light to the room, the only light left in the room came from a small lamp on his desk. He held out his hand and Lucy walked towards him taking it, following as he led her to the bed. He sat down and kicked off his shoes, patting the bed beside him. "Just let me hold you Lucy, that's all I'll do, I promise."

She sat beside him and kicked off her shoes, curling up beside him as he laid down. He took his time to adjust pillows and pull her close. "Can you tell me one more thing about your vision?" he asked softly, his breath tickling her ear.

Lucy tensed. "This isn't going to work Zeb," she insisted wiggling.

"No, it won't, not if you keep wiggling like that," he agreed.

Lucy froze, blushing.

"I can guess by the red on the back of your neck that your blushing Lucy." He kissed her softly there. "Soon there will be nothing embarrassing about this situation, and you'll be wiggling on purpose."

Lucy gasped at his direct words, but he pretended not to hear her.

"Now give me one more clue about this vision that Thomas knows so much about."

She looked over her shoulder and found his eyes only inches from hers. "You're trying to guilt me into it, what happened to only if I want to?"

"I'm not a strong man, at least when it comes to you, and I have discovered that I can be an extremely jealous man. It's a new experience for me."

Lucy reached over her shoulder and traced the red on his cheeks at his admission.

"The little girls in the vision, they weren't your nieces, they were your daughters."

His eyes grew wide at her revelation. "Were you there?" he asked as he squeezed her tight.

"Yes," she whispered, and he buried his face in her neck.

"But that wasn't all?"

"No, that wasn't all," she confirmed.

They didn't say another word and eventually, surprisingly, Lucy slept, safe and content with Zeb's arms holding her close.

Chapter 26

When Lucy awoke the house was dark, the only light she saw was coming from Zeb's computer screen. The wind was howling, and she could hear the rain as it drove sideways into the house, and she shivered at the sound of it.

Zeb had put on reading glasses and they made him look more approachable, but he was frowning at something on the screen in front of him which made him look very unapproachable.

"I didn't know you wore glasses," Lucy said in a voice rough from sleep as she sat up. "How long have I been asleep?" she asked.

"A little over four hours," he said, leaning back in his chair as his eyes looked at her searchingly.

"I'm guessing I didn't miss very much." She stretched, if she had been asleep for four hours that should make it about three in the morning, and the storm should be almost on top of them.

"I wouldn't say that." Zeb took his glasses off and threw them on the desk, and Lucy heard something in his voice that made her tense.

"What happened?" she asked, moving to the end of the bed.

"Your mother has arrived." He was watching her closely, but she hardly noticed as she closed her eyes in dread then let loose with a few words that would have made a sailor blush. Normally she didn't cuss, but her mother was definitely worth a stress relieving word or two.

"How did she find us?" Lucy asked, looking around for her shoes. "Where is she?"

"I had hoped you would be able to answer the question of how she found you. I put her in with your grandmother since you were staying here." He stood up and came around the desk, walking towards her. "I take it you're not pleased that she's here?"

Lucy snorted at the ridiculousness of his statement. "No, but I'm sure Etta was pleased to see her."

"She was," Zeb confirmed.

"Who else knows she's here?" Lucy asked. "And why didn't you wake me?" Lucy knew she would have to keep a close eye on the woman while she was here or else she would rob everyone blind. "Has she been on her own this entire time?" The idea made Lucy nervous.

"She's been with Etta." Zeb was watching he closely.

Lucy shook her head. "I'll go talk to her." Lucy jumped up from the bed and left the room before Zeb could ask any more questions. If the fact that she wasn't a social outcast wasn't enough to deter his interest, her mother would be.

She didn't bother to knock as she entered the bedroom she and Etta had been given. Etta sat propped up against the head board with a battery-operated lantern next to her, and her mother, Faith Monroe, was pacing the room like a caged animal. Lucy guessed it was because she was itching for another fix of whatever drug she was currently into.

Faith Monroe had been a beautiful young woman, she had black hair and deep brown eyes and she was small which played into her helpless routine that she usually laid on thick to get what she wanted. However, Lucy would bet that her long sleeves covered track marks and her skinniness was due to the drugs.

"What are you doing here? I told you I had no interest in seeing you the last time we spoke." She must be pretty desperate for money if she had tracked them down in a hurricane. "How did you find us, and how did you get past the road blocks?" Lucy hissed. She was unaware that she had left the door ajar or that Zeb stood outside of it watching and listening to conversation.

"Mother told me where you were, she insisted I come, I'm better now Lucy, I don't do the hard stuff anymore," Faith tried to assure her.

"Then prove it, show me your arms." Lucy waited and when Faith burst into tears and a long tirade about how Lucy didn't trust her own mother, Lucy rolled her eyes. But Lucy didn't need to see her arms to know that she was still using because she twitched and scratched, a sure sign that she was having withdrawals. She had seen it too many times as a kid not to recognize it.

"And the road blocks?" Lucy asked.

Faith shrugged. She broke one law or another almost every day, so a little road block didn't scare her.

"As soon as this storm is over you're leaving, and until then you're staying in this room with either me or Etta," Lucy insisted.

"She's not a prisoner Lucy," Etta said from where she sat on the bed.

"Yes, she is, and I'm sure she incurred several parole violations from several states just being here."

"How can you be so cruel?" Faith cried.

"The same way you've always been cruel to me and Etta, Faith. Who steals from their own mother and daughter?" Lucy ran a hand through her hair in frustration. "I don't want you here. I don't trust you."

"You don't want me to mess up your chances with the handsome man who let me in, is this his house Lucy, is he rich?" she asked with a gleam in her eyes. "You've landed on your feet, I'll give you that." Faith plopped down on the bed next to Etta. "Maybe I can get him to give some money," she suggested. "Or you can just give me some and I'll be on my way."

"I don't have any money to give you Faith, and Zeb won't give you any either." Lucy clenched her hands into fists as anger coursed through her. It was nothing new, every time something good in her life happened her mother would appear and find some way to ruin it. "And neither will Etta."

"Mama, you have a few dollars for me, right?" Faith looked at her mother with tears in her eyes but Etta shook her head sadly, and her refusal angered Faith. She rose from the bed her face red in frustration.

"Fine, then I'll just tell your handsome friend all about your secret, shall I? I'll tell him what a freak you are, and that he shouldn't trust you."

"Go ahead, tell him," Lucy said, knowing that Zeb already knew about her visions and that he didn't seem to care. It was her mother's attempt to ferret some cash out of her, and it may have worked on Lucy when she was younger, but it had no power over her now.

Faith let loose with a little scream as she charged Lucy in frustrated anger, and Lucy put her arms up to protect her face, absorbing the hits and kicks with her arms and legs. She had been through it enough times to know how to protect herself.

When the abuse ended almost as soon as it started, Lucy peeked out from behind her arms to find Zeb holding Faith back with his hand planted squarely in her chest. He wasn't hurting her, but she couldn't get past his locked arm to hit either him or Lucy.

"Enough," he said, his deep voice sending a chill up Lucy's spine as she heard the warning in it.

Lucy closed her eyes in mortification, wondering once again, how much he had heard.

Faith stopped fighting and turned on the tears. "I'm sorry, I'm so sorry, I don't know what came over me, I've been so stressed and worried about my mother and daughter." Faith started sobbing and fell on to the bed behind her and Etta leaned forward and rubbed her back. "I'm so glad that you're here to take care of them." She looked up at Zeb, her eyes huge and full of tears.

Lucy watched Zeb's hand clench at his side and the muscle in his jaw jump. He was livid, and Lucy couldn't balm him. She had brought this woman into his house.

"You wouldn't mind lending me a few dollars, would you? I need some money to get back home." She gave a delicate sniff.

"No, I won't lend you money," he said.

Faith's head jerked up, shocked at his direct refusal, men very rarely refused her anything and it confused her. She stood and walked towards him, willing to give it one more try. She placed her hand in the middle of his wide chest and gave her most seductive smile. "Oh please, just a few dollars, and then I'll be out of your hair. I'll make it worth your while."

Lucy felt sick as she watched her mother's hand fist into Zeb's cotton shirt.

Zeb placed his hand around Faith's wrist and removed her hand from his chest. "No."

And that no sent her over the edge just like Lucy's no had. She issued all sorts of threats about knowing who he was and going to the press with information about Lucy, and ruining his business, she threatened to claim that he had even given her the drugs she wanted after paying her for sex. She made all sorts of horrible threats, and Lucy sunk further and further into herself as she realized that her mother would do all of the things she threatened if she thought for a minute it would work.

"Go ahead try it and see how far you get," Zeb offered. "The three of you will stay in this room until morning, then as soon as the storm is over I'll make sure that you get where you need to be Ms. Monroe." Zeb's voice was cold and something in Lucy died at the sound of it.

There was no way he would want her now.

"Thank you, Mr. Abbott, we'll be out of here as soon as we're able," Lucy said, unable to look at him.

As he left he closed the door to the room, and Lucy couldn't help but think he was also closing the door on everything that had happened between them.

Faith started cursing and pacing as Lucy joined Etta on the bed. It was going to be a long night.

Chapter 27

Zeb was true to his word. The storm ended and everyone left by the end of the following day after all the roads had been cleared and reopened. Lucy had kept to the room with Faith until everyone was gone and then watched as Zeb put her in a car. Lucy didn't bother to ask where she was going, she didn't care.

She wanted to speak to Zeb, but with Etta wanting to go it was hard to do. She wasn't sure what she was going to find at the house, so she took Etta home first, deciding to go back to LeClair after she had dropped her off; if it was safe to leave her.

The house was fine and Shy was laying on the pier awaiting their return. Wherever he had found to wait out the storm had kept him safe. She helped Etta open the house and clean up the little that needed cleaning then she got back into her car and headed towards Zeb's house. She would gather up the rest of their stuff and talk with Zeb; apologize for her mother.

As she pulled up to the house she took her time, gathering up the courage to face the man inside. The door opened easily under her hand, almost as if the house was expecting her. She was greeted by silence and darkness, so she waited, listening for any signs of life in the house. Perhaps Zeb had left. Part of her wished that he had gone so she wouldn't have to face him.

Taking a deep breath, she started up the stairs, pausing halfway up to gather her courage once more, and as she reached his study she noticed the light and knew he was there.

Her tread was silent, and she stood in the doorway, watching him as he typed something into his computer. He looked tired and remote, and for the first time she was a little afraid of him and what he would say.

"I was wondering how long it was going to take you to make it up here, did you take the scenic route?" He leaned back in his chair and looked at her.

"No, I was nervous to see you again."

He looked at her, not saying a word, so Lucy entered the room.

"Are you afraid of me?" he asked softly as if he didn't want to scare her away.

"Not physically, but I'm afraid of what you're going to say," Lucy licked her lips nervously.

He stood and walked around the desk motioning for her to join him, and as Lucy crossed the room she felt as if the floor was falling out from under her, and when he took her hand she froze. She saw a bright light and visions, so many visions. Some of them had her and him, others had her and him and three girls, one with silver hair. They were both young, middle aged, and finally old.

"Lucy?" he asked softly, waiting for her to respond. When she looked at him she had tears in her eyes, it could only mean that he had made a decision, a decision that included her in the rest of his life.

She cleared her throat and looked away from Zeb. She needed to remember why she was there, she needed to apologize. "I'm sorry about Faith, Etta always believes her when she says she's changed. I think it's the mother in her always hoping that she has."

"Don't worry about Faith, she's been dealt with," Zeb said as he reached out and took her hand pulling her towards him.

"H-how?" Her voice trembled, but not because of the question or the answer, but because there was something different in his touch, in the way he was looking at her.

"Let's just say that I made sure the necessary authorities knew about her parole violations." He tilted her head back to look up at him. "I don't want to talk about your mother or grandmother. In fact, I don't want to talk at all."

Lucy let out a squeak. "You don't?" she asked as he wrapped one arm behind her back.

"No." Lucy watched only for a moment before her eyes closed and then she felt the shock of his lips meeting hers. His kiss was gentle but brief and her eyes opened as he pulled back.

"Will you stay Lucy? I want this to be as much your decision as it is mine."

She nodded, knowing that if she didn't she would regret it for the rest of her life.

"I was afraid that you wouldn't come back tonight. I told myself that if you didn't I would let you go, but I don't think that I would have been able to do that."

"No?"

He smiled tenderly at her question, as if he could tell that she didn't want him to talk, she wanted him to kiss her. She could feel his body pressed tightly against hers as he held her close, his heart beating as fast as hers.

"No," he confirmed as his lips claimed hers once more, his hands holding her head before they moved lower, gathering her close.

"Just you and me Lucy," he murmured as he slowly pushed her back towards the bed.

For now, she agreed silently, thinking of her earlier visions.

When Lucy awakened much later she sat up, clutching the sheet to her chest as he looked around for Zeb. It only took a moment for him to join her with a tray of food. He was wearing only a pair of blue jeans and she took her time admiring the view. He looked better under his clothes than she could ever have imagined.

"Are you alright?" he asked as he sat next to her on the bed, pouring her a glass of wine.

She nodded as she accepted it, fighting a blush. When he leaned back and pulled her close so that she rested in the crook of his arm, she relaxed as contentment washed over her.

"You had a vision right before I kissed you, didn't you?" he asked, kissing the top of her head. It amazed her that this supposedly cold man could be so sensitive and gentle.

"I had several," she admitted.

"What were they?"

She smiled secretly to herself. "They all involved you."

"What does that mean?" He tilted her head up so that she was forced to look into his eyes.

"It means that you made a decision," she explained, knowing that she had explained it to him before.

"Then you know the decision I made?" he asked.

"I think so." She nodded.

"Good, remember it. Don't forget it." His tone was suddenly serious.

"Why?" Lucy asked, sitting up quickly. She knew she wasn't going to like what she was about to hear.

"I have to go away for a while. The storm caused significant damage to the company site in Texas, and I have to go and help with the clean-up. I don't know how long it will take." He set his glass aside and took hers.

Lucy couldn't help the dread that suddenly filled her heart. She hadn't had anymore visions filled with red, but she felt like they were there, just out of reach. He was still in danger and if she couldn't see him she couldn't see the danger to either one of them. Maybe if she could hear the right words it would comfort her.

"Zeb, why?"

"Why do I have to go?"

"No, why me?" She had thought about it, he could have any woman he wanted, why would he choose her, an outcast with a troubled past and a troubled family.

"Because, you're Lucy," he said simply before taking her lips.

It was a vague answer at best that left her wanting more, but at the touch of his lips against hers she was once again lost.

She had wanted more, more that would sustain her while he was gone, but as he kissed her she forgot about his leaving, about everything but how his touch felt, how he surrounded her with something that felt an awful lot like love.

If only her gift would have told her about what lay ahead, she might have demanded more.

Chapter 28

It had been over a month since the night Lucy had spent in Zeb's arms. She had seen him off the next morning then raced home to change and report back for work. There had been a lot to do over the next week and she had fallen into bed exhausted every day, and she imagined that it had been the same for Zeb and that was why she hadn't heard from him. It was as if he had disappeared from her life. But now, a month later, she knew he was doing it purposely, and she couldn't deny that it hurt.

She tried being reasonable, telling herself that he probably had a very good reason to not contact her, but in the end, she always came back to the same answer, she had given him what he wanted, and he had disappeared. It was truly the Monroe curse happening all over again.

She was only thankful that she wasn't pregnant.

Her goal now was to finish her work at the LeClair house and disappear. She would head back to New Orleans and find a decent job to help support her and her grandmother, and if Zeb ever did return she wouldn't have to face the embarrassment of having to see him again.

Lucy parked the car and walked towards the supermarket. Her grandmother demanded that she needed to stop on her way home and pick up her favorite hot sauce for her dinner. Lucy had told her she would go at the end of the week, but she had been insistent, and when she was insistent there was no saying no to her.

Keeping her head down, she picked up a hand basket and walked to the aisle where she knew the condiments were. She only got a few side looks and no one talked to her which suited her just fine. Swinging by the dairy aisle, she picked up some creamer and few other things they needed before making her way to the checkout, picking up a newspaper and paying for her items.

As she was paying she felt a pair of eyes on her and turned to see Holden Brown watching her closely. Thanking the young girl at the checkout, who was staring at her just as hard as Dr. Brown was, she made her get away as quickly as she could, but it wasn't quick enough.

"Wait up Lucy!" Dr. Brown called out to her once he cleared the doors of the store and was in the parking lot.

Lucy pretended not to hear him and was almost to her car when he caught up to her, reaching out to grab her arm,but she side stepped him and she noted him frown at her reaction to him.

"How is your arm? You never came to see me." He looked at the arm which was covered with her shirt sleeve.

"Fine," she said, opening her car door and throwing the groceries across the seat.

"I wondered if you had heard from Zebadiah? I haven't heard from him in over a month and I'm starting to get worried."

"Why should I have heard from him?" Lucy asked, relieved that she wasn't the only one that hadn't heard from him. That meant there was a good chance that something was keeping him away. "He's a big boy, I'm sure he can take care of himself." She turned to leave.

"Wait, I wanted to know... that night, when I helped you..." He looked at her as if he expected her to know what he was talking about. "You said something."

"What did I say?" she asked with a frown. She didn't remember saying anything.

"You said, 'he's the one, you'll be happy', Zebadiah said you were dreaming, but..."

Lucy looked away, whatever she saw was a good thing, she could do the reading and give him good news, unless something had changed.

She gave a sigh, knowing he would hound her until he had his answer she reached out and placed her hand on his bare forearm and looked into his eyes. "What did you think I was talking about?" she asked. It was the right question because she saw it all before her. A tall man, a wedding cake, moving into a new house, a party where they were old and gray.

"Marry him, you'll be happy," she said, turning once again to leave, but he reached out and stopped her once more.

"How do you know about him and how do you know we'll be happy? This town is not exactly open to people who are different," he insisted, but at least he had the grace to look embarrassed by his words.

"What's his name?" Lucy asked, and Dr. Brown seemed hesitant to share it. "I'm not going to put a curse on him," she said with an eyeroll.

"Mark, Mark Peters."

"Here's the deal, you're different, but you and Mark will both be accepted. You'll make a life here and everyone will be supportive, at least publicly.

Sure, many will go home and talk about your personal preferences behind your back, and you might lose a few patients, but others will make up for them."

"Why would they accept me, they have never accepted you?" he looked confused.

"In some ways today's the world is different and in other ways it never changes. Being gay still has its challenges, but the town will look at themselves as broadminded and pat themselves on their backs for being so accepting of you and Mark because it's more acceptable now than it was. However, being a witch will never be acceptable. Your homosexuality is definable, and it only affects you directly, my gifts are a lot less definable and can affect anyone at any time, not to mention I am sometimes the bearer of bad news not good. That tends to make people fear what I have to say."

"So, you don't say anything at all?" he asked, looking at her with something close to pity.

"Oh no, I always say something and that is often what makes people hate me, especially when it's bad news." This time she did make it into her car, and she started the engine and pulled away without looking back. She didn't need Holden Brown's pity.

The drive home was a short one and Shy was pleased to see her. She spent a moment greeting him before entering the house and calling out to her grandmother.

"That took you longer than I expected," she greeted as she took the bag of groceries.

"Sorry, I got away later than I expected." Lucy grabbed the paper and moved to sit on the porch outside. The evening had cooled off and she was eager to sit by herself for a minute or two. She leaned back and took a deep breath, pleased by the news that Holden hadn't heard from Zeb either, it gave her hope.

With a smile she opened the paper, she had got it with the intention of scanning it for a job in New Orleans, but now she didn't feel in such a rush to do that. Humming, she reached down and patted Shy who sat next to her as she flipped the pages, glad that their little town didn't have nearly as much crime New Orleans did.

She almost flipped past it, she would have, if not for the photo attached. It was a picture of Zeb and Gianna. He had his hand in the small of her back as he was walking towards a car. Gianna looked lovely in a flowing gown, the photo was black and white, so she had no clue what color the dress was, she focused on the photo and the details because she didn't want to read the blurb that was next it.

She knew she had to, but she didn't want to. Taking a deep shaky breath, she let her gaze wander over to the words. "Mr. and Mrs. Joseph Beckett are pleased to announce the engagement of their daughter Gianna Beckett to Mr. Zebadiah Abbott a..." Lucy couldn't read anymore as a sob caught in her throat.

How could she be such a fool!

The only good thing was that no one but her and Zeb knew just how big a fool she really was. It was cold comfort though. She looked down at the photo once more and then ripped it out, balled it up and threw it into the water next to her.

"Lucy, dinner's ready!" Etta called.

"Great!" she said with false enthusiasm. There would be time for tears later, and there would be a lot of tears. "I'm starved!" She moved into the house, letting the screen door slam behind her. "I'm going to go back up to the LeClair mansion to work a little bit more tonight when we're done."

"Is there that big of a rush? Thomas said that the job wouldn't be complete until late fall at the earliest."

Lucy nodded. "I'm getting bored with it. I need a new challenge. I thought the city would make a good change." She tried to make it sound as off-handed as possible. "But I'm not sure, I still have some time to decide what I want to do." She dished herself up a large serving, wondering how she would be able to choke it down.

Somehow, she did, and somehow, she managed to keep up her end of the conversation, telling Etta about her run in with Holden Brown. Eventually, the dinner was eaten, the dishes were done, and Lucy found herself driving back up to Zeb's house.

She didn't turn on any lights as she made her way up the stairs to his study where she stood silently and looked around her. There weren't that many memories, but there were a few. She looked over at the big bed and slowly walked towards it.

Closing her eyes, she sat down and let the tears come, and once they started they wouldn't stop. How long she cried for she couldn't say, but she swore she heard the house groan around her as if it felt her heartbreak.

However, Lucy knew that life had to go on, so she eventually stopped crying, picked herself up and went home to sleep. Tomorrow she would work with a vengeance and finish the job as soon as possible, hopefully before Zeb returned.

Chapter 29

Zebadiah pulled his car up to the house and got out slowly, the house looked like it must have the day it was built. It was late October and Thomas's crew were down to the final details of the project. It had taken almost seven months to complete, but he had done it.

It looked like home.

He slowly walked up the steps, eager to see the changes inside as well. He wondered if Lucy had been able to keep pace with Thomas. As he entered the house he took in the warm wood and the smell of fresh linseed oil and he knew she had succeeded.

The thought of Lucy made him smile, he had missed her. It had been over two months since he had last seen her, and he had thought of her every day. She had been the one thing that kept him pushing to complete the work in Houston, and then the fiasco in New Orleans, as quickly as possible. He wanted to come home, back to LeClair, and be with her.

He took the stairs two at a time, thinking he would find her on the top story working, but the work was completed and she was nowhere to be found. Frowning, he pulled out his phone and looked at the time. It was after five, perhaps she had gone home for the day. He turned and started down the stairs with the thought of going to her house, he could bring her back here.

"Well look what the cat dragged in," Thomas said with a grin as he entered through the front door. Zebadiah looked behind Thomas, hoping to see Lucy, but she wasn't there.

"It's been awhile," Zebadiah agreed, taking Thomas's extended hand.

"Over two months," Thomas said unnecessarily.

"It looks like you've made excellent progress while I was away." Zebadiah was impatient to get to Lucy. He felt like a teenager eager to see his crush.

"We're in the homestretch now, only the detail work left." He nodded as he started to walk through the house, instantly beginning to take Zebadiah on a tour of all the work that had been done.

"And the wood work, all of that has been completed?" Zebadiah asked casually.

"Almost three weeks ago, Lucy worked like a mad woman to get it done. She had a job offer in New Orleans that she couldn't pass up, so she put in a little extra time."

Zebadiah felt his jaw tense at the news that she was gone.

"New Orleans, I don't suppose you have her contact information, I have some additional work I'd like her to do for me." Zebadiah watched Thomas as he studied his feet.

"No, I don't. She chose not to share where she was going with anyone, not even Etta. She calls to check in every now and then though." Suddenly, he looked up, his eyes meeting Zebadiah's with the fakest smile he had ever seen the man give. "I hear congratulations are in order, when's the wedding, or has it already happened? We read about the announcement not too long ago."

Zebadiah cursed silently to himself, but his face remained calm, almost cold. He had hoped the news wouldn't make it this far north. If Lucy had heard, his heart stopped at the thought of it, she would have run, which is exactly what she did.

"There was never an offer or a plan to marry." Zebadiah said shortly. He could tell that Thomas didn't believe him, meaning he wouldn't lend a hand in finding Lucy.

"The house looks great, I'll have to start furnishing it soon," Zebadiah said, changing the subject to Thomas's obvious surprise.

"Yes, I know a few people who can help you with that if you're interested," Thomas offered.

"No thanks." Zebadiah wanted Lucy to furnish the house the way she wanted to, and he had no doubt she wanted to. "What about out back?" he asked, leading Thomas out onto the back veranda to look over the new porch railings and columns.

He spent another half of an hour with Thomas before he left, and as soon as Thomas was out of sight, Zebadiah got in his car and drove to Etta's to find out exactly what was going on with Lucy. He knew she would tell him.

******

Lucy's feet ached as she climbed the stairs to the small apartment that she shared with another girl about her age. They both worked at one of the hotels in the French Quarter, and it was always busy, no matter the time of year.

She pushed through the door, which tended to stick, and entered the cold apartment. It had one little window unit to heat and cool it, and they turned it off when they weren't there. Neither one of them had much money so they were both frugal, which suited Lucy fine.

She threw herself down on the couch and looked at the pile of mail that sat in front of her on the table. She had little doubt that it was full of bills. Pushing her shoes off her weary feet, she fell over onto the couch and thought of Zeb. She couldn't help but wonder where he was and what he was doing. He was probably picking out china patterns with Gianna.

Lucy closed her eyes against the tears that threatened at the thought.

"What a hell of a day!" Paisley Denham said as she entered the apartment. "Lionel was on a rampage in the kitchen, how was the front of the house?" she asked as she plopped down on the chair across from her.

Both she and Lucy worked in the hotel's restaurant, Lucy waited tables and Paisley worked as a sous chef, but she had also been known to wait tables when she needed extra money, which was almost all of the time.

"It was a day just like all of the others, rich men and women thinking that they deserve extra service without any extra expense."

"Extra expenses like tipping the waitress?" Paisley laughed. "Been there. What we need is one of those rich handsome men to take us away from it all." She sighed at the daydream

Lucy thought of Zeb and felt her heart stop. "You know the rich ones are always a little deranged, right?" she joked.

"Sure, but to what degree and is the fortune worth the hassle?" She looked over at Lucy. "I'm not looking for true love, it doesn't exist, but money, that does exist."

"Yes, it does," Lucy agreed, thinking of the pearls that Zeb had bought her simply because she had admired them. He hadn't even blinked at the cost.

"What about Pizza for dinner? I have coupon," Paisley suggested, jumping up from her chair.

"Sure," Lucy agreed, not really hungry.

When her phone rang she jumped, the only one who had her new number was Etta.

"Etta?" Lucy couldn't keep the concern and fear from her voice.

"Lucy, I'm not doing well, can you come home for a day or two, just to help?" Etta's voice sounded quiet and rough, as if she had a cold.

"Of course, I have the next few days off, do you need me tonight, or will tomorrow morning be O.K.?" Lucy didn't relish driving down there this late. It was after ten and she wouldn't get there until after midnight.

"Tonight, I'll sleep better if you're here, could you pick up some cold medicine on the way? I'm completely out." Etta coughed.

"I will, and I'll be there as soon as I can," Lucy said, ending the call then jumping from her seat with a burst of energy. "I have to go; my grand-mother is sick."

It took her ten minutes to pack a bag and get in her car. She was lucky that she did have the next two days off otherwise she would have had to call in sick, something that was frowned upon by management.

At least Etta needing her took her mind of Zeb, even if it was only for a little while.

Chapter 30

By the time Lucy hit the city limits of Belfort she was exhausted. She had stopped for coffee and had the radio tuned to something upbeat, but none of it was helping. The expanse of long dark road that wound before her had a hypnotizing effect.

Perhaps that was why the raccoon that darted out in front of her caught her off guard, and she slammed on her breaks swerving so hard she ran off the road, barely missing a tree. It only took seconds for police lights to turn on behind her. She had noticed a car some distance back, but with the light blinding her she had no clue that it was a police vehicle.

Putting the car in park she rested her head against the seat's headrest. She was sure that the police officer had seen the raccoon and was only coming to check on her, and it would give her a minute to calm down before she continued to her grandmother's.

She turned off her radio and prepared to roll the window down, but when she saw it was Joel Bradley approaching she groaned, mentally preparing to defend and deflect as she rolled down her window, but she had no chance as her door was automatically wrenched open and her arm was grabbed as she was pulled from the vehicle.

"I should have known it was you Lucy Monroe."

Lucy was quite sure he had known it was her, which was why he had been following her.

"Have you been drinking?" He pulled her away from the car, his hand like a steel band around her arm.

"No," Lucy answered.

"It looks like you have been drinking, you ran off the road and almost hit a tree." He pulled her to the back of her car and spun her around. "Place your hands on the back of the car."

"Why?" she asked, unwilling to comply and open herself to him like that.

"Are you resisting arrest?" he demanded roughly, grabbing her arm and twisting behind her back.

"Arrest! What crime have I committed?" She fought him.

"Driving under the influence," he said, completely serious.

"This is harassment, you haven't even tested me to see if I have been drinking, which I most certainly have not!" she insisted.

But he wasn't interested as he threw her up against the car and reached for his cuffs. Lucy was really starting to get scared, it was the middle of the night and it was unlikely another car would pass them for some time. Joel could do whatever he liked to her.

It took him only a few seconds to cuff her since she was no match against his strength. He spun her around and started to pat her down, taking what felt like an unnecessary amount of time around breasts and inner thighs.

Lucy closed her eyes feeling humiliated, there was nothing she could do, she was close to tears when a car pulled over in front of hers, and her body sagged in relief at the sight of Zeb's massive form unfurling from the car. She hadn't wanted to see him again, but she was relieved that she was.

"Is there a problem here?" he asked, approaching Lucy at a steady and unhurried pace. It was too dark to make out the expression on his face, but she could hear the steel in his voice.

"This is police business, you need to get in your car and leave, otherwise I'll be forced to arrest you for obstruction of justice." Joel pushed Lucy towards the back of his squad car.

"It looks more like harassment to me, but go ahead, call for back up and arrest me," he suggested, stepping in front of the backdoor of the squad car, blocking Joel from placing Lucy in it.

When Joel tried to stop her Lucy kept walking right into Zeb's chest. Zeb stayed close, but otherwise he didn't touch her.

"I'll ask again, why are you arresting her?" Zeb stared down at Joel, expecting an answer.

"It's not my place to say, now step aside." Joel tried to pull Lucy away, but Zeb's arm reached under her cuffed arm and around her waist.

"As her legal representation, I have a right to know why she is being arrested," Zeb insisted.

"You're not a lawyer." Joel snorted his disbelief.

"I assure you I am a lawyer, and I'm sure Lucy will confirm that I am her lawyer if you ask."

Lucy nodded her head, realizing that she really knew nothing about the man that was holding her against him so tightly, but she trusted him.

"She is being arrested for drunk driving," Joel ground out between his teeth.

"What leads you to believe that she is drunk?" Zeb questioned, looking down at Lucy, looking into her clear and alert eyes. "She looks alert to me, and I don't smell any alcohol on her."

"I witnessed her run her car off the road." Joel explained, pointing to her car, which sat haphazardly on the side of the road behind them.

"It didn't have anything to do with the dead raccoon in the road behind us?" Zeb asked.

Lucy swore she had missed it, which meant that Joel had to have hit it and kept on going, and that meant that Joel did know why she had swerved and ended up on the side of the road.

"And of course, you've given her a field sobriety test or a breathalyzer test, have you even bothered to read her her rights?" Zeb watched Joel squirm.

"I'll do that at the station."

"Then I suggest you call for back-up and arrest me for obstruction of justice, and my one phone call will be to the judge to make sure that there is a court order for the video that your camera has taken." Zeb waited, and when Joel still seemed indecisive he continued, "or you can let Lucy go and we'll forget the whole thing, because you and I both know she isn't drunk."

Joel muttered something under his breath as he undid Lucy's cuffs. "Fine, but I want her to prove that she's not drunk, I want her to do a field sobriety test," he insisted.

Zeb gave a short nod in agreement, looking down at Lucy, making sure that it was alright.

"He won't have to touch me again, will he?" she asked, shuddering at the memory of his hands running over her body.

"No, it won't be necessary," Zeb assured her coolly, but she saw something close to rage flare in his eyes.

Lucy nodded and stepped away from Zeb, glad that he was watching as Joel led her through the test. When it was over he turned and walked away, getting into his car and driving off without a word.

Lucy stood on the side of the road, rubbing her wrists, now that the ordeal was over she started to feel the chill of the October night seeping into her bones.

"Are you really a lawyer?" she asked, not knowing what else to say. What did one say to an ex-lover? It was a new situation for her. She hadn't heard from the man in over two months, and as if she had conjured him up suddenly, he was there to save her.

"Yes, it was my first career choice, but when my father grew ill unexpectedly I had to step in and take over the family business, and it turned out that I was better at that than I was at being a lawyer."

"I don't know, you seemed like a very good lawyer just now." Lucy took a deep shaky breath, realizing that it could have gone so much worse if he hadn't of shown up when he did. "How long have you been back?" she asked.

"I got back this afternoon, I just finished having dinner with Holden Brown and was on my way home," he explained.

Lucy nodded, her eyes narrowing at the coincidence of being called home on the same day he returned. "Have you been to see Etta?" she asked suspiciously, she swore she saw his lip twitch at the question.

"I stopped by looking for you." He smiled but didn't say anything else.

"How did everything go in Houston?" she asked, walking back towards her car, not wanting to prolong the conversation. He didn't seem in a hurry to be on his way, but he wasn't exactly falling to his knees begging her forgiveness or sweeping her into his arms telling her how much he had missed her.

"It got sorted, along with a few other problems that occurred in New Orleans," he assured her.

"I'm glad," and then because she was a glutton for punishment, "I heard about your engagement. Congratulations." She was pleased at how steady her voice sounded considering how her heart was shattering as she said the words aloud.

"What if I told you there was a story behind that?" he asked, stepping towards her.

Lucy took a step back, bumping up against her car, she turned to open the door. "I would say that there almost always is." She paused needing to hear him say it.

"But it is true, are you engaged?" she asked, coming directly to the point.

"I never agreed to it?" he said vaguely.

"What the hell does that mean!" Lucy insisted.

"It's a long story and you're tired. I'll catch up with you soon and I'll tell you all about it." He held her door for her and waited as she sat behind the wheel of her car. "Are you alright to drive home?" he asked.

"Yes, it's not that far." Lucy said, a little dazed at his simple dismissal of the subject.

Didn't he care? She felt the anger start to simmer as she asked herself the question.

"You sure you don't want me to follow you?" he asked

"Yes!" she said behind clenched teeth, her anger suddenly swelling to rage. He was concerned now, but where was all that concern over the past two months?

"You're simply lovely when you're angry," he said, dropping a quick kiss on her lips before closing her door for her.

Then she watched, astounded, as he walked away without a backward glance, got in his car and drove away. She wasn't sure what she expected, an explanation, a denial, a guilty apology maybe, but not a vague dismissal of the subject and a parting kiss as if he would see her tomorrow and it would all be fine.

Even though it almost gave her hope that it would.

Chapter 31

The hotel had called a brief meeting for the restaurant staff, and Lucy was sitting at a table in the back with Paisley, who was being chatted up by a new waiter named Dean.

While they waited for the management to arrive, Lucy thought back to her quick trip home the previous week. Etta hadn't been awake when she had arrived, and she had seemed slightly off the next day, but nothing that worried Lucy overly much. The house had needed a good cleaning and there had been plenty to do, so she had stayed to get it done.

She had also stayed with the hope that Zeb would track her down in order to explain his comments to her, but he never did, and Etta didn't mention his return. It didn't appear as if there had been a plan between the two of them, which was a little disheartening.

What could he have meant by saying he had never agreed to an engagement? It had been posted in the paper, how could that have happened without his agreement?

She remembered how it had felt when he had held her close, keeping her safe from Joel, and she frowned at the thought of Joel, hoping that she wouldn't have another run in with him anytime soon. He seemed to be getting nastier every time she saw him.

"What are you thinking about so hard over there?" Dean asked. He was a tall skinny young man who liked Paisley but was guarded around Lucy.

"Nothing much." She shrugged, looking away from him.

"I hope they get here soon," Paisley said. "I got Lionel to agree to let me come to this meeting, but if it takes much longer he's gonna be livid." She popped a bubble with her chewing gum, giving Lucy the impression that she didn't particularly care.

Lucy had always thought the temperamental chef had a thing for Paisley because she got away with a lot more than everybody else did.

As if he had heard Paisley's request, the manager of the restaurant, Mr. Bernstein, walked in with a few women, one of which was Zelda Abbott. Lucy sank further down in her chair, hoping she wouldn't be noticed as the manager began to talk about the annual Halloween Ball that was being held in the ballroom of the hotel. The restaurant was catering, which meant that it was a great chance for some of the staff to get overtime.

If Zelda noticed her she didn't give it away as she stood next to two women that Lucy didn't recognize.

It was a short meeting, and they were soon released to return to work or their time off, and the manager moved with the women to a table at the back of the restaurant, implying that they were about to have lunch.

The table was in Lucy's section.

"Hey Paisley, can you take the manager's table? I need to call my grandmother and check on her." Lucy said.

"Sorry, no can do, Lionel will kill me." Paisley looked over at the table and gave a mocking smile. "Besides, this is your chance to get in good with some of the upper crust of New Orleans. Of course, the only one at that table worth talking to is Zelda Abbott."

Lucy followed close on Paisley's heels as she walked towards the kitchen, wanting to ask her what she knew about Zelda.

"You better get over there, the manager looks anxious." Paisley grinned, ducking into the kitchen.

Adjusting her apron over her uniform of a starched white shirt and black slacks, she walked towards the table.

"Hello Mr. Bernstien," she said to the manger as she smiled at the table as a whole. Zelda met her eyes and returned her smile, giving her a little wink, but otherwise not saying a word, and relief washed over her.

There would be no need for introductions or explanations.

They gave her their drink order and said they would all dine off the buffet. It would be an easy table for her.

After she retrieved their drink order she darted back to the kitchen, cornering Paisley.

"What do you know about those women at the table?" Lucy asked, hoping that Paisley ran true to form and would let loose with all of the gossip that she had.

"Not much, my mother used to work for Zelda's father when I was little, and Zelda was always nice to me and would let me play with her things on occasion. I had the biggest crush on her brother. He was in graduate school at the time." Paisley paused with a far away smile on her face. "He was something."

"And?" Lucy prompted after a few moments with nothing more.

"There was some sort of scandal surrounding their mother, she was mixed race I think. Mr. Abbott did all he could to protect her, but in the end she left because of it. I'm not sure of all of the details, but it kind of rocked the rich white people's world at the time, and not in a good way."

Lucy forced herself to keep her mouth closed as she absorbed the news. It wasn't enough, she wanted more, but she didn't want to ask Zeb, she wondered if Zelda would share?

"I used to have such daydreams about Zebadiah Abbott, Zelda's brother, I wonder if he's as good looking as I remember? He would definitely be one of those rich men I would let carry me off into the sunset." She sighed.

Realizing that she had to go and check on her table, Lucy exited into the restaurant and was stopped by Zelda as she rounded the buffet.

"Lucy, can we meet?" she whispered urgently. "I agreed to something I shouldn't have, and I think it may have hurt you and Zebadiah, he's not at all happy with me right now. I'd like to explain."

Lucy nodded. "I get off at seven this evening, would you like to meet here?"

Zelda shook her head. "No, here's my card, can you meet me at this address?" She passed the card over to her quickly.

Lucy nodded, pocketing the card before moving away from her, towards the table, checking to make sure that there was nothing else they needed. After that she had a few other tables arrive and they kept her busy, so she didn't have another chance to talk to Zelda before she left.

There was a lull about half past two, and Lucy took her lunch break with Paisley and Dean. Dean kept looking at her funny.

"Is there something wrong?" Lucy asked, as she took a bite of her sandwich.

"No," he insisted as he kept watching her as they ate.

When Paisley left them to return to the kitchen and Lucy stood, Dean slid his phone over to her. "Is this you?" he asked.

Lucy looked at the photo of her with Zeb at the gala, her face going pale, but she neither confirmed or denied it. However, Dean took her lack of response as an affirmation. "I almost didn't recognize you, if it weren't for the hair I probably wouldn't have." He looked her up and down. "What happened, why the fall from grace?"

Lucy didn't respond as she turned to walk away. When Dean reached out to grab her she side stepped him, she didn't want him touching her, and she wouldn't look at him.

"You're hiding something!" he insisted.

"No, I only went on a date with a rich man." She shrugged.

"I remember that night, I was part of the wait staff, he bought you a very expensive strand of pearls." His eyes were glued to her.

"He may have bought them, but they were not given to me." Lucy turned to walk away.

"You're lying. I wonder what the press would think? I can read the headline now, 'Abbott's mistress slaving away as a waitress as he picks out china patterns with his bride to be'. I'd read that."

Lucy shook her head, walking away from him. If she responded he would think there was more to it then there was, but she couldn't help but be nervous about his threats. She had tried to warn Zeb that he should stay away from her, but he hadn't listened, and now it seemed he was going to pay for it.

Perhaps she could warn Zelda and she could warn Zeb. She looked at the clock on the wall, she had three more hours until she could get away, she wondered if he would try to call in the tip before then, she had fifteen minutes left in her lunch break.

Making a decision, she walked out onto the terrace of the restaurant, which was empty, and pulled out her phone, dialing the number on the card that Zelda had given her.

"Zelda!" she greeted when she heard her voice, "I need to talk to Zeb, it's urgent, do you have a way for me to get in contact with him. I have a new phone and I don't have his number stored in it."

"Sure, he's here with me now, hold on." She heard Zelda's muffled voice and then Zeb's voice was talking in her ear, and she closed her eyes as she let the warm sound roll over her. It was an automatic comfort, he would know what to do.

"Zeb, I think I'm about to cause you trouble," she said softly.

"How so?" he asked, his warm voice sounding amused.

"There's a waiter where I work, and he recognized me as your date from the gala. He's planning to go to the press with a story saying I'm your mistress and your keeping me on the side even though you're engaged," she said it all in a rush and was greeted by his silence.

"How are you Lucy? I miss you," he said.

"Zeb, did you hear what I said!" she hissed.

"Hmmm, yes. You know all I keep thinking about is the night you spent in my arms. I shouldn't have left, or I should have taken you with me."

He was playing some cruel joke.

"Stop it, just stop it!" she choked, as his words spread through her, warming her soul.

"Zelda said she's going to visit with you this evening, you are still coming?" he asked.

"Are you going to be there?" She cleared her throat, praying the answer was no. She didn't think she was strong enough to see him again without throwing herself into his arms.

Damn it, she had to remember she was mad at him.

"Would you like me to? I can be."

"No!" she swallowed hard at the thought.

"I wanted to explain, but Zelda said it would be better if she did. I don't suppose you would be my date for the Halloween Ball?" he asked in an about face, completely throwing her.

"No, I have to work, I need the money," Lucy said without thinking.

"Fine, but I'll find you Lucy." There was a pause and when Lucy didn't say anything he sighed. "I hope you have a good visit with Zelda."

"Goodbye," she said quickly, not knowing what to say. He had twisted her all up inside and she wasn't sure if she was mad or happy. They were the words she wanted to hear, but it still didn't change the fact that he was engaged and he shouldn't be saying them to her.

She hoped whatever it was Zelda had to tell her would help her make sense of it all.

Chapter 32

Lucy pulled up into the drive of the massive house in the Garden District. Her little beat up car had never looked as out of place as it did now. There were lights on in the house giving it the appearance of warmth, but she had her doubts that that's what she would find.

The slamming of her car door sound abnormally loud in the evening quiet, and giving a little shiver at the chill in the air, she headed towards the front steps of the house, but before she could get to the top the door opened and Eden flew out of it and threw herself into Lucy's arms.

Lucy couldn't help but smile, it was a very warm welcome, and any awkwardness there would have been was lost in Eden's chatter as she took her hand and led her into the house.

It was all marble and glass with a large chandelier in the open foyer and only a center table to greet visitors.

"Thank you for coming," Zelda greeted, talking over for her small daughter as she led the way into a formal living area that looked like something off the cover of a magazine. "Eden, sweetie, go play upstairs for a little while, I need to talk to Lucy for a few minutes."

Eden started to protest, and Zelda gave her a stern look. "We talked about this Eden. Lucy will come and see you before she leaves.

Lucy watched Eden leave the room with a dramatic pout then sitting on a small sofa when Zelda motioned that she should.

"Would you like something to drink or eat?" Zelda asked as an afterthought.

Lucy shook her head, only wanting to get to the point of why she was there.

Zelda gave a shaky sigh and sat across from her. "Zeb found the shooter."

Lucy jerked at the news, she hadn't known that he had shared that bit of information with Zelda so it was not what she expected to hear. "When? How?"

"Summer's boyfriend."

"He was the shooter?" Lucy asked, it took her by surprise, but it made sense, especially after the vision she saw. "Is Summer alright?"

Zelda nodded. "Thanks to you. Zebadiah had someone keeping an eye on her when her boyfriend lost his mind...but let me start at the beginning."

Zelda closed her eyes and organized her thoughts, looking for the best place to begin.

"After the storm Zebadiah went to Texas to take care of some business there. He needed Summer's help and he arranged for her to join him, but when she didn't make her flight he was concerned. It's not like Summer to just not do something. He had a bodyguard watching Summer and, after a little digging, he discovered that it had been a few days since anyone had heard from him.

"Zebadiah was irate that something that important had slipped through the cracks, but with the hurricane..." she shrugged. "Summer had gotten away thanks to the bodyguard's quick action, and she hid out in a hotel for a few days before she got the nerve to call me. Unfortunately, Gianna was with me when she called, and she overheard the call."

"What happened to the bodyguard?" Lucy asked, afraid to hear the answer, expecting the worst.

"He was hit over the head and stuffed in the trunk of his car. He spent over twenty-four hours in the trunk." Zelda stood up and started pacing, and Lucy guessed that the next part was the bad part.

"I went to pick up Summer from the hotel where she was hiding out after calling Zebadiah to let him know that she had called. He had a few of his security team go with me and Gianna insisted on going as well. When I arrived Summer was beside herself, she was convinced that the bodyguard was dead and it as all her fault. She proceeded to tell me and Gianna about how her boyfriend had lost his mind when he had heard that she was going to meet Zebadiah in Texas. He had threatened to kill Zebadiah and Summer, and admitted to already attempting too shoot him once but missing. He said he had followed her to Zebadiah's house in Belfort and had seen them together after the gala. Summer denied it, but he didn't believe her."

Zelda turned to look a Lucy. "I asked him who he was with and he said that it was you and that you had been shot that night. When Summer found out she was terribly upset."

Lucy nodded not sure what she should do or say.

"Gianna came up with a plan, she thought that Summer would be safe, and that her boyfriend might believe Summer more readily and be less of a threat if Zebadiah was suddenly engaged."

"And of course, she was willing to pretend." Lucy snorted, and Zelda blushed.

"It seems ridiculous now, but we were all so scared. Some of the threats her boyfriend made against her," Zelda shuddered. "It seemed logical at the time."

"When Zebadiah found out what we had done he went through the roof, and he was forced to return to sort out the mess that we had made trying to protect Summer. He laid into me and Gianna, primarily out of concern that you would find out about the fake engagement and believe it. Which you did. Now, in hindsight, I don't doubt it was Gianna's plan all along, to get rid of you."

"Zeb still could have found me, or called me and told me what was going on at any time," Lucy insisted.

"He wanted to, but I convinced him that it had already been done and it would be senseless to undo it, at least until the man was caught and locked up, and if Zebadiah tired to seek you out it might actually put you in danger. I also told him that a week more wouldn't matter, and that you probably hadn't even heard anything about it."

"When it was all done, and he did return and learned that you had heard about it he was angry at himself for listening to me. It's not something he does often, and he was reminded why." Zelda frowned.

"You know, the only other person to call him Zeb was our mother. He wouldn't allow anyone else too, but he lets you." Zelda sighed, sitting next to her on the sofa. "Many people think he's a cold man or harsh, but he really has a huge heart. Over the years I've watched and waited to see who he would give it to, or if he would give it to anyone at all. Part of me always thought he would settle for someone like Gianna."

Lucy attempted to take in all that Zelda had said, especially the part about Zeb giving his heart away, if he had given it to her, as Zelda had implied he had, he had never let her know about it.

Realizing this was her chance to ask her about her mother, she took a deep breath. "May I ask you a personal question?"

"Sure, I think I owe you that, at least." Zelda gave a self-mocking smile.

"Today, someone told me about your mother, could you tell me a little bit more?"

"Paisley?" Zelda asked.

Lucy nodded.

Zelda shrugged. "There's not much to tell, our mother's mother was Native American and African American and her father was Irish. She was beautiful and she married my father who adored her. The people in my father's world never accepted her, she was a bit of a social outcast. Thinking that she was hurting Zebadiah, me, and my father, she left and returned to her home town where she wasn't treated much better. I never had any interest in building a relationship with her, but she and Zebadiah were close, especially towards the end of her life."

Lucy had a feeling that there was much more to it, but Zelda either didn't know or didn't want to share so she didn't push.

"I begged Zebadiah to let me talk to you first so that you could see it was all my fault and none of it was his." Zelda stood, and having said her piece, her guilt was lessened.

The only problem was that Lucy didn't agree. It wasn't all her fault, she still felt that Zeb could have called her and told her, she wouldn't have shared the information, and it would have made little difference to the out come of the situation. Lucy sensed that there was something that Zelda didn't know about and the only person who did know was Zeb.

Zelda's phone rang, and she answered it, after a few short words she handed the phone to Lucy. "I'll go get Eden, you don't mind spending some time with her, do you?"

Lucy shook her head as she took the phone, knowing it was Zeb.

"Hello," she greeted, watching Zelda leave the room.

"Did what she say make a difference?" Zeb asked, his voice warming her like it always did.

"No."

She could hear the smile in his voice. "I would have been disappointed if it had. I have a feeling that I need to do a little explaining and groveling. Will you at least let me do that now?"

Lucy smiled. "I'll think about it and let you know."

"Promise?"

"I promise. I'm glad that Summer is safe, that you found the shooter, and that you're safe too," she said, and when he went to say something else she quickly told him goodbye and hung up. It would be too easy to forgive him, and she had a lot to think about before she did.

Chapter 33

Lucy was working the lunch shift once again and the restaurant had been busier than usual, something she was grateful for because it didn't allow her to think too much about what had happened the night before. She still had plenty of questions that she wanted answered, the primary one being why he hadn't bothered to call her.

Did he think it was going to be that easy to sweep back into her life?

"You seem to be a little distracted today," Paisley said as the stood together at the serving station.

"Is it that noticeable?" Lucy asked wryly

"Yes, is it your grandmother? Is she ill again?" Paisley asked as she garnished a few glasses of tea with lemon wedges.

"No, it's-"

"Oh my God, lucky duck!" Paisley interrupted her with a nudge and a nod in the direction of a table in Lucy's section.

Lucy's gaze followed the direction of her nod and saw Zeb being seated at a table. Why was he here? Did he know she was here? He had to know, Zelda had to have told him where she met her yesterday.

"That's Zelda Abbott's hot brother, the one I was telling you about yesterday. A bit of a coincidence, don't you think?" Paisley eyed him as she picked up her tray. "He's even better now that he's older, he looks far more commanding and a lot more mysterious."

Lucy shook her head at Paisley's comment. The only mysterious thing about him was why he thought he could walk back into her life so easily.

"Remember to smile, he's filthy stinking rich, and even if he doesn't offer you forever he'll probably leave a good tip!" she joked as she hurried away with her tray.

Dean slid into the empty place she left. "He generally doesn't offer his mistresses forever, but I'm sure he'll leave you a good tip," he said nastily.

Ignoring him, Lucy walked slowly towards Zeb's table. He was looking at his phone as she approached, but when he sensed her arrival he lifted his head and let his gaze linger over her. Lucy could feel the heat of it all the way to her toes.

"What can I get you to drink?" she asked. To ask him why he was there would only encourage him.

"I'll have a sweet tea with lemon please," he requested, looking back down at his phone.

"Is the guy who's been threatening to go to the press the one you were just talking to?" he asked, throwing Lucy. She hadn't thought he had noticed her, much less who she had been talking to.

"Yes," she said softly, looking over her shoulder to where Dean was watching them.

"Have you decided to agree to let me try and explain?" He changed subjects once more. It was making her head spin once again, she would swear he was doing it on purpose.

"Maybe," she hedged.

"It will take a little bit longer than a passing conversation, at least the length of a dinner," he insisted.

She turned to go get his drink without responding, and he reached out and grabbed her arm lightly, with a finger only, but it was enough to make her stop.

"Please Lucy," he begged. "If you're still of the same mind after my explanations I promise, I'll never approach you about it again."

Lucy felt a little spark of anger. "Do you even realize why I'm so angry?" she hissed, leaning into him.

"Yes."

"I don't think you do!" She shook her head, tears threatening. She had given him something she had never given another man, her innocence, and he had taken it and then left without a word. It wasn't even the farce of an engagement, at least it wasn't anymore. She got that, she understood what had happened and that none of it was his doing. But he hadn't attempted to contact her for two months.

He read the hurt in her eyes and when he attempted to reach up and touch her face she jerked away. "I'll go get you your drink and return to take your order." She turned on her heel and headed back towards the serving station.

"Trouble in paradise?" Dean mocked before he picked up his tray and moved away only to be replaced by Paisley.

"It looks like you caught his attention." She gave Lucy the side eye, unable to miss her flushed cheeks.

"Was he hitting on you, do you want me to get Lionel?" she asked.

Lucy shook her head, seeing how it would appear that way, he had detained her and then attempted to touch her face.

"Did he use the 'you have a bug on you' line?" she asked. "I have to say I never took him for one who would push himself on a woman, he wouldn't need to." Paisley kept looking at her, hoping for an explanation.

"It's fine," Lucy assured her. It was all she could say. Picking up Zeb's drink, she carried it over to him and then walked away to check on a few other tables that she had. She was back at the serving station, refilling drinks with Paisley and Dean both beside her, when he approached them.

"I can't stay," he said, smiling at Paisley before turning his attention to Dean. He looked him over, taking in every inch of his appearance. The warning was evident in his look, he didn't need to say a word.

Dean turned red and swallowed hard before scurrying off.

"Was that really necessary!" she said between clenched teeth. Looking up at Zeb who was watching Dean's retreating back.

"Yes," Zeb's cold eyes turned to her, "he got the point."

"He did, and now he will probably try to do something for sure Zeb!" Lucy stopped what she was doing and frowned at him.

"Then I'll deal with it. Can I take you out to dinner?" His eyes met hers with a silent plea.

Unable to say no, she nodded her agreement, telling herself she wasn't caving exactly, she was giving him a chance to explain.

"Good, I'll pick you up at eight?" He dropped a quick kiss on her lips.

"Stop! You're going to get me fired!"

"I doubt that," he said dryly, turning to leave.

"You don't know where I live," she called out softly.

"Yes, I do." His grin made her heart stop and she heard Paisley sigh behind her.

"Zeb uh, you guys know each other?" Her curious gaze followed Zeb as he left the restaurant.

Lucy shrugged. "I did some work on his house and we went out a few times."

"Why didn't you tell me! He must have come here to see you. That's a sure sign that he likes you."

"I never doubted that he liked me." Lucy shrugged. She knew he liked her, but did he want her, forever?

She couldn't keep denying that she wanted him, in fact, she was in love with him. Her eyes closed at the thought. What a time to admit it herself. She had seen the visions, she had had strong feelings for him from the beginning, but she had never admitted that she loved him, at least not to herself.

She had been too afraid.

"What was up with Dean?" Paisley asked, looking at him over her shoulder.

"It doesn't matter." Lucy was too tired to explain. Picking up her refills, she carried them over to her table and had to work hard at soothing the irritation that her delay in delivering them had caused.

But all the while she was trying to figure out exactly when she had fallen in love with Zeb and if there was anyway he could ever love her back.

Chapter 34

Lucy was late getting off from work. It was as if everything had been against her all day. When she raced home and entered her apartment it was to find Zeb sitting across from Paisley. Paisley looked a bit frustrated and, even though Zeb was wearing his aloof look, Lucy picked up on an underlying current of amusement from him as he and Paisley stared at each other.

"I'm sorry I'm late, I'll only be a few minutes, do I need to dress up?" she asked, hoping the answer was no. Lucy looked at his informal state of dress and realized that it would be easy for her to match, but she was relieved when he confirmed her guess with a shake of his head.

She raced around her room, discarding her uniform and reaching for a pair of jeans and a soft cotton t-shirt with a light sweater. She was changing out her shoes when Paisley entered her room, throwing herself on the bed with a pout.

"I tried to steal him, but he wasn't interested." She watched Lucy as she stood and moved to the mirror above her dresser to check her hair. "Then I tried to get him to share what was going on between the two of you, but I couldn't crack him"

Lucy smiled at the idea of anyone cracking Zeb. "I would have been disappointed if you had." She reached for her wallet, keys, and phone, shoving them into her pockets. "There is nothing going one between us," she insisted.

"That's not what Dean said, he said that you were Zebadiah's date to the annual Abbott Gala and that he bought you a very expensive strand of pearls."

Lucy rolled her eyes. "I was there as his friend and he had to buy something, he does every year. I did not get to keep the pearls, have you seen any pearls around here?" Lucy demanded, her anger getting the better of her. "Dean's a rat who is trying to make trouble for Zeb by going to the press with his lies."

Paisley held up her hands in surrender. "O.K mama bear, I believe you, but I will say that you must care a little to be so upset about it."

"Of course I care, he's my friend!"

"But that's all?" Paisley asked, watching her closely.

"That's all!" Lucy confirmed, turning and leaving her room in a rush. When Zeb stood as she entered the living room, she couldn't help but admire the way he filled out his jeans and t-shirt, and the leather black jacket he wore gave him a rebel vibe. Lucy had a feeling that she had just jumped from the frying pan right into the fire.

"Are you ready?" he asked as she joined him.

She couldn't speak so she nodded and headed for the door.

"I won't wait up!" Paisley called as Lucy closed the door behind them.

"Your roommate is..."

"Annoying?" Lucy supplied.

Zeb grinned, letting his guard down, she could actually feel the change in him. "Enthusiastic."

"Nosy."

"Curious."

"She said she hit on you and was upset because she couldn't get you to talk," Lucy watched his reaction to her blunt words.

"She did, and it was very flattering, but it would take a lot more than an annoyingly enthusiastic and curiously nosy roommate to break me." He led the way to his car, opening the door for her as she laughed at his witty reply.

He caught her face with his hand and dropped a quick kiss on her lips. "Thank you for giving me a chance to explain," he said, and all she could do was nod in reply, breathless at his intense look. "There's a lot I want to say..." Lucy watched as he struggled to find the words and she felt her heart melt. "I am sorry that I hurt you."

She looked up at him and took a shaky breath. "Let's go get something to eat and talk about it."

He nodded, and she could see his shoulders relax as he closed the door. The smell of leather seats and Zeb enveloped her, and she leaned back into her seat, letting it sooth her.

The restaurant Zeb chose wasn't far from his house. It was a little hole in the wall pizza joint and Lucy looked it over as they pulled into the parking lot. "Is this so you won't have to be seen with me?" she asked before she could think better of it.

"No, this is one of my favorite places and I wanted to share it with you," he explained, not sounding angry or hurt by her comment. It was as if he realized she wanted him to prove something, although Lucy had no idea what that might be.

When they entered the restaurant, Zeb was greeted by everyone there, confirming that he did indeed eat there a lot.

"I'm sorry Zeb, that was a mean thing for me to say," she apologized as they were seated.

"I get it Lucy," he said, and she knew that he truly did.

They settled in as their waitress came over, looking surprised that Zeb had a guest with him.

"I've never brought anyone here before," he explained as Lucy realized that they were getting similar looks from the other staff. "I suppose that I should have asked you if you like pizza," he mused aloud as he watched her look over the menu.

"Sure, I like pizza," she said setting the menu aside. "Why don't you order your favorite," she suggested. Once that was done they looked at each other in silence and Lucy had the feeling that Zeb was trying to figure out where to start.

"Tell me about your mother?" she suggested.

"My mother?" he looked surprised at the request.

"Is that why you took a chance on me, decided to trust me, because I reminded you of her."

"Your situation reminds me of her, but you don't. I would say that watching how people treated her based on her heritage, not who she was, taught me not to judge people based on what others think, but I wouldn't say you remind me of her."

"No?" Lucy asked wanting more, "I'm a little relieved, after hearing Zelda describe her...situation... I thought that you might have some deep seated need to save me because you hadn't been able to save her." In for a penny in for a pound, if they were going to be honest she might as well start, and it was something that had been weighing heavily on her since she had learned about her the previous day.

"My mother didn't need saving." Lucy watched his face grow distant and she was sorry that she had opened that door. "She married my father and he adored her, but she didn't care for him the way he did her. I loved my mother, but her life had made her hard. She had been taught the hard way that the only one she could rely on was herself, and she only really loved herself. It was a relief when she left. The few times I visited her in her hometown, I was confused about why she had wanted to return, but as I grew up I realized that those in my father's circle didn't treat her any better. It was a case of the devil she knew."

Lucy nodded, she got it, how many times had she used that same excuse to stay in Belfort. The world could be a scary place. "But she left you and Zelda. I don't understand how a mother could just leave her children."

"That's one of the ways you're not like her. I watch you with Eden, you're both crazy about each other. My mother never had that type of relationship with either me or Zelda, perhaps it was because she never got it at home, or maybe she just wasn't meant to be a mother, not all women are. I do believe that one of the main reasons she left was because she thought her heritage was hurting us, and if she was out of sight it would be out of mind." He shrugged. "All I can say is that you are so much more than she ever was, but I'm thankful she was my mother because I learned a lot from her."

It was the most that she had ever heard talk about himself.

"But she is the reason you chose not to judge me despite what others told you?"

"Yes, and I'm glad I did-"

Lucy thought he was going to say more but their food was delivered, putting a stop to their conversation while they served themselves and started to eat.

"Why didn't you call Zeb?" she asked softly after a few minutes.

"The first few days were due to lack of ability because of the storm, but when I was able to get and receive messages there were a few very disturbing ones waiting for me, and I didn't know who they were from. All I knew was that whomever was sending them was smart enough to get a hold of my personal information, which isn't easy, and I knew that you were alone with Etta and there was no one to protect you. No one knows about us, and I was afraid if I called you it would alert whomever was making the threats and it would make you a target as well."

Lucy thought it over, it made sense it was just the sort of noble thing he would do.

"I wasn't overly worried because I only thought I would be a week, seven days tops, and our conversation before I left led me to believe that you understood, you said your visions showed you my decision."

"But Zeb, all it took was for you to change your mind, make another decision and those visions could have easily changed!" She clenched her napkin in her fist, angry once again that he didn't get it, so she decide to let him have.

"I gave you something I never gave any other man, to share that with you and then just have you leave...I thought you had gotten what you wanted so you were done with me, part of me still wonders if that's the case and you're only back for round two." She couldn't hold back the tears as she looked away from him.

He reached across the table the took her chin in his hand, forcing her to look at him. Lucy was surprised to see tears in his eyes too. "I'm sorry Lucy, I'm sorry to have put you through that, but I would do it again if it meant keeping you from danger. All I thought about was you, I wanted to come home and hold you again, but I didn't dare. You had already been hurt once because of me, and I swore I would never let it happen again, and I won't. I would sooner die having you hate me than to ever see you hurt again."

"But you hurt me Zeb!"

"It's not the same thing Lucy, and I pray to God that you can forgive me, but I won't take it back. Summer's boyfriend was delusional, even Gianna was a fool for getting involved, but better her than you because it kept you safe."

Zeb took her hands in his and looked into her eyes. "Tell me what you see Lucy?"

"I don't see anything Zeb." She shook her head.

He stood up and reached for her, pulling her close. When his lips landed on hers she gave a little cry and then lost herself to the feel of his kiss.

Then the visions came, so many of them all at once, they were the same as before but more vivid, stronger. When he pulled away he looked down at her. "Do you see them, are they still there?"

She nodded, and he pulled her close.

"Will you come home with me Lucy?"

All of her visions were still there, she would trust herself and go with him.

"Yes, but we still have more to talk about."

"We'll talk all night if that's what you want." He threw some money on the table then wrapped his arm around her and led her out into the cool evening.

She still doubted him and she prayed she was making the right decision.

Chapter 35

Lucy followed Zeb into his house and into the living room, she was relieved that it wasn't his bedroom. It seemed she was bound and determined to underestimate the man at every turn, maybe she was part of the problem. He had begged her to remember her visions while he was gone, but as soon as he was away from her she had lost her faith in him.

But how was she supposed to act when she read about his engagement to another woman?

"Would you like a drink?" he offered.

Lucy shook her head and moved to the window that looked out over the garden. She couldn't see much but it gave her something to do.

"Would you like me to start at the beginning?" he asked, sitting in a chair next to the fireplace, drink in hand, watching her.

"That would probably be best," she agreed, turning to join him. Sitting across from him on the couch as she grabbed a pillow and held it close, unsure if it was for comfort or protection.

"The first time I saw you?" he suggested.

"Zeb, not that far back!" Lucy rolled her eyes.

"No, I think that's the perfect place to start." He leaned back in his chair. "You had a vision, several if I recall. I didn't have a vision, but I felt...excitement, I was intrigued and then instantly jealous when Thomas pulled you aside. You looked shocked with your first vision," he looked at her.

"That was the one where I saw you with the two little girls." She nodded.

"Our little girls," he said softly, and Lucy felt a thrill zoom through her at his words, "what haven't you told me about the vision?"

"I was pregnant, we were taking the girls up to bed and I was following behind you, making sure the little one didn't fall down the stairs, and you were making me nervous as you lifted the oldest over your shoulder, making her giggle." It seemed so real to Lucy, more now than it ever did. She remembered that she had felt that they were in love.

"I heard little girls giggling." He smiled at the memory. "I thought it was Cecelia and Gianna. What was the second vision, the one where you grew pale?"

"That was the one where I saw red and you fell backwards." She shivered as she remembered.

"And the third vision, the one where you blushed. I loved watching you blush, it was charming. I have wondered ever since then what you saw to make your cheeks that red." He gave her a devilish grin and Lucy blushed again.

"I saw us," she cleared her throat, "we were in a big bed surrounded by white."

"What were we doing Lucy?" he asked, his eyes darkening.

Lucy blushed again. "I'll leave that to your imagination."

He laughed. "But not for long I hope."

Lucy's blushed deepened.

"The next time I saw you, you were all alone in that house, anyone could have come by and hurt you." He frowned at the memory.

"The door was locked," she defended herself.

"Yes, but the house is so large, and you were wearing headphones, I doubt if you would have heard a window break, and Bradley showing up the way he did only proves my point." His eyes drilled into hers, trying to get her to admit that he was right. "Feeling protective of another person was new to me. I have never felt that way about anyone else before, but there is something about you that makes me feel it." Lucy watched his hand clench around his glass. "When I saw Bradley touching you the other night, it took every ounce of self control I had not to hurt him." Lucy watch a shudder course through his body. "The thought of someone hurting you, of you being hurt, it almost brings me to my knees." His eyes met hers and she could see the truth of his statement.

"From the moment I met you I knew I wanted you, but I didn't know how bad until you turned me down. Then, as I realized how innocent you were, I hated myself for suggesting it."

"But you don't hate yourself for taking what you wanted and then leaving me?" she asked, unable to hide the hurt and fear in her voice.

"I didn't take what I wanted, it was, thankfully, given willingly, and I didn't leave for good. I was coming back as soon as I could, and if that dolt of a sister of mine and her friend hadn't started playing games, I would have been back much sooner. I was always coming back, but by the time I thought it was safe to call you I couldn't get you on your phone, and the words I miss you and I love you were not something I wanted to pass on through someone else, damnit!"

Lucy froze, she actually stopped breathing at his words.

He continued as he rose out of his chair. "You fascinate and frustrate me because no matter how hard I try I can't get a grasp on what you're feeling or thinking. I'm generally self-assured and know what I want and how to get it, but with you that all goes out the window. You make me feel like a damn kid who doesn't know whether I'm coming or going, and I'm nervous as hell every time I ask you out that you'll say no, and you often do!" He was yelling by this point and Lucy was crying happy tears as he said all the words she always wanted to hear.

He made her feel powerful and wanted.

"I feel like I'm the luckiest man in the room when I enter it with you, and I want to destroy everyone who has ever hurt you and can't see how wonderful you are." He pushed his hands through his hair in frustration. "And jealous, every time I see Thomas with you it's like a punch in the gut that he knows you better than I do!"

"Not in every way Zeb," she interrupted him, walking towards him, placing her hands on his face. "I love you too, and I'm so scared that this is some crazy joke. I should have trusted the visions, I should have trusted you, you've never given me a reason not to. But it's hard and I don't trust easily. Why would a man like you want me?"

"Because you're-"

"Lucy," she finished for him. He had finally stopped yelling. "The funny thing is that everyone talks about how cold and hard you are, even you, but you've never been that way with me. I see a very passionate man who is unbelievably generous and kind and accepted me when no one else would. You believed in me and I'm so sorry I didn't believe in you." She was truly crying, and he held her close.

He looked down at her and kissed her hard, looking deep into her eyes. "I do love you."

"I love you too," she said, her voice breaking.

He smiled gently. "And I forgive you for not trusting me..." He waited, his eyebrow arched.

"You're forgiven for taking what you wanted and leaving and not calling me for two months," she agreed. She knew he wanted her to apologize too.

"Why do I have a feeling I'm forgiven but it's not forgotten?"

"Oh, it won't be forgotten, and I reserve the right to remind you of it for the next fifty years at least."

"That sounds like a plan, you're lovely, will you go to the Halloween Ball with me?" he asked

"You always do that!" She all but stomped her foot as he traced her face lovingly.

"What?"

"Throw me for a loop by throwing in a bunch of compliments around a serious discussion then asking me something off the wall!"

He nodded, not really agreeing or disagreeing with her take on what he was doing. "I thought we could dress up like Prince Charming and Cinderella."

"So long as Cinderella is dressed like a waitress because I promised to work."

"Fine my silver eyed witch, you work and I'll play, but for the record once we're married you'll never have to worry about money again.

"Zeb," she said. His comment reminded her of her mother and the trouble she could cause between them. "My mother-"

"Not something I'm worried about in the least."

He kissed her hard making her forget about all of the things they had yet to discuss, there would be plenty of time, a lifetime.

"You'll stay?" he asked.

"Yes, unlike some people I know, I'll stay, but if I do leave I'll call every once and awhile."

He picked her up and threw her over his shoulder.

Somehow she got the feeling he was done talking.